A GANGSTA'S QUR'AN 3

Romell Tukes

Lock Down Publications and
Ca$h
Presents
A GANGSTA'S QUR'AN 3
A Novel by *Romell Tukes*

Lock Down Publications

P.O. Box 944
Stockbridge, Ga 30281
www.lockdownpublications.com

First Edition December 2020
Printed in the United States of America

Lock Down Publications
Like our page on Facebook: Lock Down Publications @
www.facebook.com/lockdownpublications.ldp
Cover design and layout by: **Dynasty Cover Me**
Book interior design by: **Shawn Walker**
Edited by: **Nuel Uyi**

Stay Connected with Us!

Text **LOCKDOWN** to 22828 to stay up-to-date with new releases, sneak peaks, contests and more...

Thank you!

Submission Guideline.

Submit the first three chapters of your completed manuscript to ldpsubmissions@gmail.com, subject line: Your book's title. The manuscript must be in a .doc file and sent as an attachment. Document should be in Times New Roman, double spaced and in size 12 font. Also, provide your synopsis and full contact information. If sending multiple submissions, they must each be in a separate email.

Have a story but no way to send it electronically? You can still submit to LDP/Ca$h Presents. Send in the first three chapters, written or typed, of your completed manuscript to:

LDP: Submissions Dept
P.O. Box 944
Stockbridge, Ga 30281

DO NOT send original manuscript. Must be a duplicate.

Provide your synopsis and a cover letter containing your full contact information.

Thanks for considering LDP and Ca$h Presents.

Acknowledgments

First and foremost, all praises are due to Allah for blessing me with an amazing talent, thank you to all the loyal readers, thanks to all the good men behind the walls in these prison yards pushing me. Letting me know I got the juice. Shout to my Yonkers and Peekskill team Smoke black. Killer from the Skills, Fresh, CB from O back, Spayhoe, King Hand, YB, Cruddy Gang, and Smurf. To my Philly Bulls Musa, Big C, Legs, and Dime, Tony N.C. fa, Lil B, Twerk, Big Ray, Capo, and Shoota. Shout to my muscle Gang Team, my Brooklyn fam Tim Dog, K, Skrup, Bonafide, Black Knowledge A-Team, Big Will, Green Eyes and DaDa, my Flat Bush fam and of course, my BX fam you know who you be. Big shout to LDP for this amazing journal and opportunity in the game; I'll always be beholden to you. Stay tuned—more heat to come from me.

Romell Tukes

Prologue

South Beach, Miami

It was a nice hot summer day on the beach. Ali was enjoying the hot sand. He wore a pair of blue Versace swimming trunks with no shirt, showing his well-chiseled frame from lifting weights five days a week. Lil Ali was building sand castles with some other kids he just met. They were enjoying the summer as the guards were all separated throughout the packed beach. Two years ago, Ali's life was flipped upside down, leaving him with a lot of deep, open wounds. Ali's gaze moved from the crystal clear water into the bright skyline that made Miami a sight to behold.

***

Two Years Prior

Musa brought Ali into his underground society after Ali beat some murders. Musa had moved him out to Vegas with his daughter—Laura—who was deadly in love with Ali, and they got married months later. Musa was a head member of *The Firm*—a powerful organization that ran almost every casino in the Vegas and Tri-State area.

When Musa died, Ali took his seat within the organization as everything went left. The Mob families tried to muscle Ali and his crew out of the picture. This caused a big war with Ali and the Mafia families.

Ali went to war, using tactics that were unheard of—from extortion, kidnapping bosses of rival organizations, killing their families, and outsmarting the Mafia.

What he didn't see coming was, going to war with his own brother—Haqq—who tried to kill him on Christmas. Luckily, Abu Hurayra's daughter—Ayesha—saved him. Ali killed Haqq, and ensured the opening of his new casino in the Middle East—with the help of Jacob, Musa's son.

Musa's other son—Rome—was killed by Joker, the Mexican Mafia leader who also recruited D-Bo—a childhood friend of Ali—to help him set his plan in motion.

Before Sofia killed her father—Santana—he sent killers to Ali's home, and they ended up murdering his wife, Laura, and his OG—Akbar.

Chapter 1

Aguadilla, Puerto Rico

Sofia Santana drove in the back of all-pink custom made Rolls Royce Dawn, with the window curtains closed and blocking out the dangerous contaminated streets of Rincón, where a category four hurricane recently hit.

Lots of people died from dehydration and dysentery; so Sofia donated food and millions of dollars. She also helped rebuild a lot of homeless people's property.

She ran one of the most treacherous Cartel families in North America, since she had her daughter Cristal who was the spitting image of her father— Ali.

She still kept her daughter a secret from Ali, but she prayed she would be able to tell him one day, and not lose the only man she'd ever loved.

Last time she saw Ali, she date-raped him by slipping him a mickey in his drink.

Clad in a yellow tight Fendi dress, Sofia was on her way to her private jet to visit Moreno in Cuba. She hated dealing with him, but they were somewhat business partners.

Once at the private landing strip, there were three black SUV trucks with sixteen G-27 gang members patrolling the area with high power rifles.

The driver had been speeding the whole ride, almost waking up her daughter who was sleeping in her lap.

"Enjoy your trip," the Spanish driver said as two guards opened her door; then one of them took Cristal, bringing her inside the jet.

"You too," said Sofia. She then pulled out a blue plastic Glock, shooting the driver six times in the back of his skull.

Sofia grabbed her Fendi bag and placed her Fendi sunglasses over her face, strutting inside the jet as all the guards eyed her phat ass that was fake but looked amazing.

***

Miami, FL

Ali saw Lil Ali having so much fun on the beach he didn't want to stop him, so he was planning to give him twenty more minutes.

Ever since the death of his mother—Mona—and his wife—Laura—because of his beef with the Mafia and the Santana Cartel, he was left alone to raise a boy into a man. Haqq's son—who was Ali's nephew—had been living with his grandma since his mother and father died.

Miami was a new start for Ali. It was a beautiful city with beautiful women and lots of money. His CMA casino was financially planning to open next month. Jacob was running the Middle Eastern casino which was raking in a lot of money.

Ali checked his gold Sky-Dweller Rolex watch, realizing it was past two p.m. and he had an important meeting with investors in an hour.

"Lil Ali, come on, it's time," Ali said, tucking his 9mm.

"Come on, dad, ten more minutes," Lil Ali said, running towards Ali with sand all over his face, hands, and the rest of his body.

"No, you need a shower," Ali said, handing him his shirt.

"Okay, I guess," Lil Ali said in his six-year-old voice. Lil Ali scratched his long braids full of sand just to get rid of the itch.

Ali walked past groups of beautiful women dressed in bikinis showing a lot of ass and skin. The city was very bi-culture, so a person would see all types of foreign bitches who looked really exotic. His five guards were twelve feet away on Ali heels, watching everyone—as they did 24/7. Ali phoned up an investor.

"Daddy, daddy! Ice cream, please!" Lil Ali yelled, tugging his father's arm, pointing at the ice cream truck on the curb.

"Okay," Ali said, giving him a fifty dollar bill, and he ran to the ice cream truck surrounded by kids and parents. Ali was going back and forth with the investor because he was trying to buy a club, and the investor was trying to tell him the owner increased the original price.

Ali was so busy arguing with the Jewish man he took his attention off his son because the guards were sitting on the sidewalk, watching the crowd.

Lil Ali finally made it to the truck window as the ice cream man looked at him.

"Can I have two cookies and cream cones please? And you can keep the change, Mister." Lil Ali was getting his father ice cream, and being generous as his father taught him.

When Lil Ali handed the man the fifty dollar bill, the weird-looking man snatched Lil Ali's whole arm, pulling him in the truck window as two masked gunmen started to shoot through the crowd at Ali and his guards. Ali's goons were already shooting at the moving truck. Two gunmen were shooting two AR-15 assault rifles out the back of the speeding ice cream truck, hitting two luxury cars

Ali hopped in his Ferrari 488 Spider, trying to chase the ice cream truck that was long gone as civilians and two of Ali's guards lay dead in the streets.

He rode through the chaos, looking for a ice cream truck, but came up empty-handed.

***

Cienfuegos, Cuba

Moreno was in his mid-fifties slim, dark-skinned, blue-eyed, and 100% Cuban. He was soft spoken and a super freak. He loved sexy women. Sofia especially made his dick hard every time he saw her big ass, big tits, and sensuous curves.

He lived on twelve acres surrounded by his 12,171 square foot mansion and his farm where he raised cattle, horses, chickens, and hens.

Sofia and Moreno sat outside under his gazebo, as the gray clouds formed as if it was about to rain. This was Cuba's everyday tropical climate.

"Do you have any idea who we're up against? I don't believe you do. Well, let me tell you, this fuck killed every active Mafia crime family from Boston to Vegas. We can't let him take over what me and your father worked so hard for." The Cuban Cartel boss paused and looked at his army of trained soldiers posted up around his stone mansion.

Moreno couldn't help but look at Sofia's thick thighs, wondering if she was wearing thongs because the way her ass jiggled when she was walking earlier drove him crazy

"First off, my eyes are not there," Sofia said, pointing at her breasts, where Moreno's gaze was fixed on. "My father is gone, so personally I don't give a fuck what you are or were to him but I run the show now. Let me handle Ali when the time comes."

"I'm trying to protect my investments. I don't want this potential threat to spread like a wildfire then it blows up in both of our damn faces. Learn the business, it's not pretty."

"I understand but we don't have enough manpower in Miami to go to war with a man like Ali. He's smarter than you think."

"How do you know?" Moreno asked suspiciously.

"Because I do, I'll be in touch," Sofia said, leaving.

Romell Tukes

Chapter 2

Vegas

Fatal stood with mixed emotions over the grave of his wife—Brittany—and his daughter—Kelly. He was soaking wet in his Marc Jacob raincoat over his three-piece suit. It had been hard to get over the murders of his lover and daughter. Even after killing Venny, he still felt the pain and sorrow. Never in a million years would Fatal think Venny would kill his own daughter and grandchild because he was black.

Since Ali was in Miami, and Jacob was in Israel, he chose to stay in Vegas. He had taken over the casinos. Shit was smooth since the Mafia families were either dead, or skipped town after Ali put the fear of death in their hearts.

Fatal had his own crew from his hometown in Vegas with him—Gorilla and hundreds of Blood gang members pledged their allegiance to the big homie Fatal.

Life was moving so fast. Fatal remembered when he was in Attica prison yard in New York years ago cutting niggas faces over the phone.

Now he was wearing Balenciaga to exercise in, and pushing different color Wraiths every day of the week. Fatal heard footsteps behind him, causing him to reach for his handgun as he heard the heels come to a stop.

"You okay, baby? You been here for a while, I'm just coming to check on you," Amber said, placing a Dolce & Gabbana umbrella over him.

"I was just leaving," he told his new lover.

"I don't want to rush you; I just ain't want to be alone," she said in a soft sweet voice, as they walked off to the

Wraith parked next to a GMC truck full of shooters from Brooklyn.

Amber was a bad bitch born and raised in LA with a middle class family. She attended college at Michigan State, and she received her Law degree at the young age of twenty-four.

Instead of becoming a lawyer, like most of her class-mates, she became a model ripping the runways from London, New York, Japan and Italy.

She was 100% Polish—a five foot nine voluptuous white girl with a nice tan, blue cat eyes, brown, shoulder-length hair, small waist, and round ass. She had full lips, big DD breasts, flat stomach, long eyelashes, thin waxed eyebrows, and a Colgate white smile.

Fatal met her at a fashion show for Jimmy Choo in Hol-lywood last year, and he fell in love with the Megan Fox look alike.

To get her name and number, Fatal ran down on two gay designers and pistol-whipped them until he had everything he needed to know about Amber.

A week later, Fatal saw her at another fashion show. He approached her, telling her how hard it was to get in touch with her. He even told her about what he did to the two gay designers. She'd already heard about that incident, and found it hilarious now that she heard if from him directly. She considered him cute, but crazy.

After a couple of dates, she saw he lived a very expen-sive lifestyle: luxury cars, private jets, flight club status, jewelry, expensive suites, security guards, and personal chefs.

When she saw his condo, she knew he was a drug lord. When she asked him about his line of work, he laughed. His laugh got her mad because she really liked him, but she was against drug dealers.

Her parents would disown her if they found out she was dealing with a drug dealer and a black man. It could be even worse because he was her first black guy.

When Fatal brought her to the casino, she was confused because she didn't gamble; but when he explained to her that he ran the casino, she was relieved that he wasn't a Jeff Fort.

She fell in love with his Brooklyn swag and his muscular body. His big dick had her talking to God every night, and he was a real caring man.

Weeks after they got intimate with each other, Fatal told her what happened to Britt and Kelly, and she felt so bad for him.

Sometimes at night, he would wake up in cold sweats and scream for Brittany and Kelly. Amber didn't want to take Brittany's place; she just wanted to bring happiness to his life.

***

Mossad, Israel

Amina and Jacob lay naked in bed in their skyrise apartment that looked over the beautiful foreign city. They lived on the same block as the USA and French ambassadors' offices.

"Damn, you so wet," Jacob whispered in her ear, playing in her wet pussy that was extra tight.

"Bend me over and fuck me—" she moaned, as he did what she asked.

He slowly rubbed her small waist as he slid the head of his dick into her wetness, between her nether wet lips, thrusting back and forth until Amina caught a rhythm, her tight walls loosening up.

"Ugghh, shitttt—Yessss—I'm cummmingggg!" she screamed, as she filled his cock with her creamy juices while he went deeper, making her scream at the top of her lungs.

When he pulled out, Amina slipped between his legs and started licking and sucking his dick. The more he moaned, the more she went crazy on it.

"Mmmmmmm," Jacob squirmed, as she increased the friction of her lips on his penis while she bopped up and down like a pro.

Amina let the vibration of her throat tease him before pulling back to suck the tip of his dick, as his fingers coiled around her long hair, and then he played with her nice perky tits.

"Fuck, babe—I'm about to cum."

"Oh, hell naw—I gotta get mine and I want it now," she said, taking his dick out her mouth. Amina grabbed the KY jelly, and rubbed some in her asshole and on his hard dick dripping out pre-cum.

"Fuck me in my ass," she said, bending over again, spreading her soft ass cheeks.

Jacob licked her tiny brown asshole. She moaned from the sensation. He slowly entered the groove of her ass and then penetrated her tiny brown hole, causing her to tense up. "Uhhmmmmm, fuck m-e-e-e—" she moaned, inhaling sharply, flooded with intense pleasure as he slid in and out her tight back door; and she took that dick, throwing back against it. She bumped back and forth, grinding ferociously against him.

"Ahhh ugg—" she screamed, feeling his dick all in her ass, as she came back to back while he continued to pound her ass hole as if it was her pussy.

"Don't stop, daddy—" Amina moaned, with her asshole now wide open, as he finally came in her. Then he pulled out as cream poured out her asshole.

"Damn, nigga, I ain't know you was feeling as spiritual as I am today because my soul has been touched by God," she said, her thighs trembling as copious cum was all over her ass cheeks and bed sheets.

"Let's take a shower, I gotta go to work and you're going to the other casino, so I want to see you all day," Jacob said, seeing it was 6:35 a.m.

"Yeah, so I want round two," she said, smiling, following him into the marble floor bathroom with gold sinks, toilets and a gold shower.

The couple had been in Israel for two years now. Amina had even become a Muslim, something she always wanted to do but was scared of being judged by many.

She had grown used to wearing a hijab and Muslim garment all day. An hour later, Jacob was fully dressed in a Tom Ford suit. Amina wore her Muslim outfit, trying to walk straight because her ass hurt.

"Why are you looking at me like that, baby?" Jacob said, seeing her stare at him through the mirror.

"Because I want a ring—I hate having sexual intercourse without being married; it makes me feel uncomfortable," she replied honestly, sitting down.

"Give me some time, I will marry you, trust me. I love you. Come on, I have a meeting at the Aftab Casino."

"Okay, I'ma text you, baby—I love you," she said, as they both left.

Romell Tukes

Chapter 3

Miami, FL

Ali stood on his condo balcony overlooking the west south beach environs, unable to think straight since last week when his son was kidnapped. Lil Ali was the only immediate family he had left, and he was gone in a blink of an eye, and Ali only blamed himself.

Nobody got a good look at the ice cream truck driver and his accomplices, so he didn't even know where to start looking for the kidnappers.

Ali walked back into his crib to see his large photo of Malcom X above his fireplace in his living room that read 'by any means necessary' at the bottom of the photo.

Two of Ali's guards were killed, alongside a couple of civilians that comprised kids and elder women. The police were going crazy trying to find the shooters, but they came up empty-handed; it was all over the news. They didn't have a picture of Lil Ali; they just said a little boy was kidnapped, unaware of who he was or who his parents were because he was taken before the police arrived.

Ali wore a Gucci robe with slippers, sitting down on his white leather couch as guards surrounded the condo which was worth $12.7 million.

The condo was 9,747 square feet, with four bedrooms, three bathrooms, a family room, grand architectural floors that were so shiny a person could see their own reflection. The kitchen had top-of-the line appliances, and there was a fully stocked bar in the dining room area next to the 1.2 million dollars' chain cabinet.

Miami had respect for Ali and his crew, and they knew the boss wouldn't stop shedding blood until he found his son.

Ali had Miami's best shooter on his side, a nigga named Haitian Boy, who was a legend in the 305.

He couldn't even think, so coming up with a plan wasn't his best option at the moment until he got himself together.

Lately, he had been drinking heavily. It was his way of dealing with the pain. He went to pour himself a drink, as his guards went inside the family room to play the game systems for money.

Ali answered his phone that was ringing on his living room table.

"Long time no speak, Mr. Ali," the familiar voice of Sofia said through the phone as he frowned.

"What the fuck do you want?" he answered back, not in the mood for Sofia's games as he thought about their last encounter when she drugged him and raped him; by the time he realized what was going on, it was too late. Her pussy was so good he just wanted to cum.

"I need to speak to you right now. It's very important, no goons, no games. I know it's been two years but this isn't about us."

"I don't have time right now, I'm sorry."

"Yes, but I do have time. And you must create time because I'm downstairs coming up. So tell your guards to let me in, please."

"Two minutes then I want you out—come to the penthouse," Ali said, hanging up and calling his guards, telling them to let Sofia in and to wait outside.

Sofia walked through the hallway to see ten guards posted up in suits staring at her in her blue Givenchy dress showing her crazy body, as all of them were dreading.

She knocked on Ali's double doors to hear Ali's goons whispering and staring at her phat ass.

Ali opened the door and walked off. She saw he had long silky dreads covering his face. She saw how big his muscles got, and her pussy got wet as she closed the door with her daughter who was asleep in her arms. Sofia followed him into the polished condo that smelled like cherries.

"Nice to see you, Ali," she said, as he turned to face her for the first time. Sofia saw his red evil eyes, strong jaw, and hurt in his eyes; she could feel his danger. His energy was off, as she sat down with Cristal in her arms.

"Where is my son?"

"What! What are you talking about?" Sofia replied, confused, as he looked at her awkwardly for any signs of dishonesty.

Ali knew how dangerous Sofia was; she robbed him years ago and killed her own father for his clout and success.

"My son was recently kidnapped,"

"Oh, my god! Ali, I'm so sorry. I had no clue. Damn, Ali—"

"Why are you here to show off your baby?" Ali said, looking at the cute baby sleeping in a Hermes baby outfit.

"This is Cristal—our daughter, Ali," she said, as Ali finally saw the baby's green and hazel eyes staring at him. The baby woke up at that moment.

"Excuse me—How? We never—" Ali paused and remembered two years ago.

"Yeah. I'm sorry about how it went down, but it is what it is. I don't expect you to be a father. We are good. You have your own issues. I just wanted you to see your daughter."

"Ummmm—" he said, zoned out.

"I also came to talk to you about opening a casino on my turf. Ali, you're about to cause a lot of problems. This isn't Vegas or Philly. You can't just move in on people's areas and take over without a fight. I run the Santana Cartel and Moreno is my ally. Please just find another location. I will find one for you." Her voice rang with passion all the while she spoke, but Ali kept mute, giving her a blank stare.

"Okay, I'm leaving because I see you're not in the right state of mind. We may have history, Ali, but I can't let you destroy my empire." Sofia stood to leave, taking his silence as a declaration of war.

"Can I hold her?" Ali asked, as Sofia was walking out with her daughter.

Although she was pissed off, Sofia repied Ali in the affirmative. "Yes." She handed Cristal to her father. She saw her daughter smile so hard her dimples looked like tunnels. Her daughter looked so happy in Ali's muscular arms Sofia didn't realize she had tears in her eyes when Ali handed her Cristal back. Sofia rushed off and cut his condo down the hall. Once inside the elevator, she broke down in tears, realizing how much she still loved him; but she couldn't show emotions because if Ali opened his casino, Miami would turn into a bloodbath.

***

Durango, Mexico

Joker was addressing his henchman—Spyder. "I need you to go to Cali to speak to the Mexican Mafia about the new shipment of weapons I plan to send them. I just need you to make sure we have no slip-ups like last time."

"Alright," Spyder said in his cowboy outfit and matching boots.

"I also have a shipment going to D-Bo, so inform him. I hate that monkey but he makes us a lot of money."

"Of course that's why he's alive; he is your bishop that will help you make checkmate," Spyder said.

Joker ran the Mexican cartel. His crew was top five—one of the most dangerous cartels in the world; they killed police, tourists, government officials and other Cartel families. The most powerful Cartel family was the Gomeze Cartel, and Joker hated them. Joker and Spyder walked through the small farm, heading back to his mansion surrounded by his army.

***

Bridgeport, CT

D-Bo walked around his 13,817 square foot mansion, which possessed five rooms, three bedrooms, a six-car garage, two pool areas, an exercise room, and a basement game spot for his crew all from the D.C. area.

Since Joker had been supplying him, he'd become a millionaire. He now was a major plug in D.C., Delaware, New Jersey, CT and Westchester, NY.

Last year, D-Bo had a big fallout with the Southside crew after he told them he was now working for the Mexican Mafia.

Butter J was upset because he had a new connection—Abdul—in Philly, but D-Bo was banned from Philly, so he was going a separate way.

Butter J had a new crew since J Mo and Prime were dead. Man-Man was the new face of Philly even though he was from Oakland, Cali.

D-Bo loved his new rich life. He took private jets overseas, attended big parties, and drove every new luxury car, and he rolled with a pack of hungry wolves.

Romell Tukes

Chapter 4

West South Beach, FL

Lil Snoop was lying in his king-size bed with two beautiful exotic women, and one of them was his wifey—Sexy Diamond.

The two met Carla, an exotic Cuban woman, in Club Live last night, and they had been having an orgy since.

Sexy Diamond's real name was Diamond. She was one of the baddest in the city. She was half Haitian and 50% Trinidadian. Diamond was dark-skinned with smooth shiny complexion, long jet-black hair, hazel eyes. She was five foot four and thick with 36-28-40 measures. Her looks were accentuated by her chinky eyes, and there were tattoos all over her ass.

Her brother—Haitian Boy—was the deadliest nigga in Miami. Haitian Boy loved his little sister. Most would think she was a stripper or a sac chaser, but Diamond had her own cars, home, college degrees, and a good job.

Diamond was naked, sitting on Lil Snoop's face as he ate her pussy so good she couldn't stay balanced. "Uhmmmm yesss—" Diamond moaned, holding on to the head board.

Carla was on the lower section on the bed, sucking Lil Snoop's big massive dick which was the biggest she ever saw. She sucked his hard dick like a wild animal in heat. She was deep-throating most of his dick until she felt like gagging.

"Mmmm, suck that dick," Lil Snoop said while Diamond's juices covered his face and dreads. He loved the feel of Carla's mouth on his dick. Carla had dirty blonde curly hair, bronze skin, dark eyes, big firm breasts, nice phat pussy, and a long tongue. She was a bottle girl in Miami's hottest clubs, trying to make a living, raking in $1,000-1,500 a night.

Carla tickled his heavy balls with her warm tongue while jerking the tip of his massive dick. Lil Snoop arched his lower back, shoving his dick deeper in her throat while Diamond was grinding on his face, about to cum.

"Oh, shiit! Imm-m-m cumminngggg!" Diamond screamed, as her cream poured into Lil Snoop's mouth like milk.

Seeing Diamond cum so hard made Carla bob her head faster up and down while playing with her clit as Diamond got behind her.

Diamond ate Carla's pussy so good she climaxed twice within sixty seconds. Carla was still hungry for dick, and she sucked Lil Snoop more and more.

Lil Snoop loved the sounds of the loud slurping from Carla's head game, but was ready to fuck Diamond's pussy.

Diamond was still eating Carla's sweet pussy when Lil Snoop spread her ass and started to fuck her brains out, as her big ass clapped on his thighs.

"Ugghhh, oh my god! Fuck—" Dimaond groaned as Lil Snoop was killing her little dark tight pussy.

"Yess—I'm cumming!" Carla yelled, rubbing her nipples as Diamond sucked on her clit. Carla came in her mouth, as Diamond's thick soft lips still sucked on her clit. Carla was shaking, about to cum again. She spread her arms while she squirted across the room, as Diamond moved her face against the gushing pussy.

"Ugghh, fuck me, daddy—I'm cumming!" Diamond yelled, as her body was being pounded back and forth until she and Lil Snoop came.

The three made love for another hour, Lil Snoop fucked Carla in her ass; she was yelling all types of shit in Spanish as she climaxed out of her ass four times, while he ripped her tiny brown hole. Carla wanted more and more, but Diamond kicked her out after paying her two thousand dollars. However, Carla told her she didn't want the money, adding that she wanted to be a third wheel. Annoyed but amused, Diamond pushed the crazy bitch in her face. Lil Snoop guided Carla out, and told her he and Diamond would request her presence another time.

***

Hours Later

Lil Snoop was driving his white McLaren 720S Spider on his way to Lil Haiti to holler at his right-hand man—Haitian Boy.

Lil Snoop moved to the 305 two years ago to fuck with Ali. He'd relocated because he was sick of Philly, but he still visited from time to time.

Since settling in Miami, he became Ali's enforcer—along with Haitian Boy who was the craziest nigga he ever met. When Lil Snoop saw Diamond with Haitian Boy one day when they all went to Miami Heat basketball game, he was gone from her beauty and class.

When he asked Haitian Boy about her, he told him that's his little sister. Diamond just asked who Lil Snoop was. After that day, they linked up and went on a couple of dates; and it was history. From then on, they were inseparable.

***

Lil Haiti, Miami

Haitian Boy was posted on the corner with thirty Haitians sporting palm tree dreads—which was a Miami thing. The crew all had guns and drugs on them. Haitian Boy had filled those thick blocks with Haitian and Trini flags everywhere.

There were five donks sitting on 28-inch rims and other old-school cars with sick print jobs and custom designed interior, blasting hood music mixtapes.

Haitian Boy was the king of Miami. He was the connect. He ran crews in Lil Haiti—his hold—Liberty City, Carol City, Apopka, Eatonville, Overtown, Porky Projects, the whole Dade County.

When people crossed the bridge that separates South Beach from the Southside of Miami, they see two different worlds.

Born Layfetay Greancye in a small island in Trinidad called Port Lisas, where life was rough for him and his sister, their father was murdered by local robbers for ten dollars his father received from work one day on his way back home.

At the age of seven, he moved to Miami with his mother, and his little sister—Diamond—who was six at the time.

After he and his family had settled in the USA as legal immigrants who had sailed from the Caribbean, his mother got a job as a house cleaner in the Coconut Grove area.

With no education, Haitian Boy embraced the streets at the young age of fifteen, working for the Cubans—June and Moreno—who showed him the game.

By the young age of seventeen he had over twenty bodies counted for, and more than double attempted murders. He eventually caught a triple homicide outside of Porky Projects.

June had the best lawyers in town. After a year and a half fighting the case, Haitian Boy beat the case—thanks to June.

Three years ago, Haitian Boy cut ties with the Cubans because he was fucking a bad ass rich Spanish bitch who was throwing him keys of coke.

Months later, he found out the woman he'd been fucking was Moreno's wife. Haitian Boy even got her pregnant, but she got an abortion because he forced her to.

When Moreno found out it was Haitian Boy fucking his wife, he put a bag on his head—one million dollars—for someone to kill him. Things weren't so lucky for Moreno's wife, whose body was found floating in a lake.

There was a big war in the city between the Haitians and Cubans, leaving hundreds dead on both sides. The city had the highest murder rate, just like the 80's.

Months later, both men had a sit-down and called it a truce. Moreno had no clue Haitian Boy was a real gangsta, and they couldn't do anything to him because he became too powerful.

Now Haitian Boy supplied Miami. His plug was his uncle in Trinidad. He used to cop from Rome; that's how he met Ali years ago on a yacht party for bosses only.

When Ali relocated to Miami, Haitian Boy rolled out the red carpet for the big homie and joined forces.

Haitian Boy let his little cousin—Dead Eye—handle all the drug shit, while he just lived life watching out for the Feds who were on his tail for years. With Lil Snoop as his right-hand man, the two became brothers; they were similar in many ways.

***

North Miami

Ayesha just got back to her apartment from her morning workout in the nearby park she went to every morning to run, do squats, burpees, stomach lunges, and sprints.

She took a shower and washed her hair, preparing for her day. She had been in Miami for a year and a half now. Her father stationed her there to watch Ali and his investments.

To this day, she'd never had a conversation with the man she feared and masturbated to daily.

She heard about his wife's death. She felt sad for him, but she knew it was a part of the game. Ayesha loved Miami, the beaches, clubs and the night life. She met a lot of guys, but she was still a virgin at twenty-six. She still looked like an eighteen-year-old, though.

She met a couple of girlfriends in Miami. The girls—Kim and Penny—were from outta state New York and Washington respectively, and were rich kids. She told them she was a freelance writer.

Ayesha got out the shower, oiled up her sexy body, and wore a red Miu Miu bikini. She threw on an oversized T-shirt to go to the beach with her girls. Ayesha grabbed her keys to her new pink Audi R8 and rushed out.

Chapter 5

South Philly

"Say, bruh, I wonder why everytime I'm down here, some bootsy ass nigga be acting all suspicious and shit!" Man-Man said to one of his workers, while they posted up in the parking lot of Roosevelt Homes Projects on this warm spring day, as winter was dying down.

"The bull good, cuz, he be copping a half of key," Lil Larry said as he handed Man-Man a brown bag containing the forty thousand dollars he owed him. Larry continued; "He from Lewisburg. Niggas don't like coming to Philly to cop weight. Take a look at this infested shit. I mean, I'll be scared too."

"You're right about that," Big Marky said, leaning on his black Dodge Hellcat, looking around the dirty project to see friends, trash, and young goons running everywhere through the projects.

Man-Man was in control of the project. He had look-outs, snipers for the ops, and everybody was eating.

Man-Man was born and raised in East Oakland, California, but he would come to Philly to spend time with his cousins—Fat Boy and Prime—when they were alive; so he was always down with the Southside Crew. The whole Philly loved Man-Man because he was a cold-blooded killer. He killed a lot of kingpins in the city, and he was a hardcore Muslim. He was twenty-seven years old, short, brown-skinned, with long dreads, a goatee, and a swag like O-Dog from 'Menace to Society'. He wore all designer clothes, heavy chains, and Rolex watch to stunt. He had a Raider chain that matched his Raider hat.

Man-Man and D-Bo had beef. He was the one who banned him from Philly. He swore if he saw him he was going to slide down on him with 100 rounds.

"We gotta holler at the homie soon," Big Marky said. He was Man-Man's second-in-command.

Big Marky was six foot six, weighing three hundred and twenty-seven pounds—all muscle. He just came back from playing college football at Ohio State University, but was expelled for selling ecstasy to the white kids on campus.

"Okay, I'm about to slide, bruh—I got hella shit to do," Man-Man said, walking to his old-school 1968 all-silver Chevy Nova with white leather seats sitting on 30-inch rims. Big Marky hopped in his Hellcat to follow him, as Lil Larry went back in the jet with his goons to catch a dice game in the hallway.

***

North Philly

Butter J was behind the tints of his new all-black Benz AMG GLE G3 SUV outside of his car wash, watching the nightfall.

He saw a teenager barely sixteen pushing a baby carriage alone with bags tied to the handle. Butter J shook his head, glad he just sent his sister off to college. All three of his sisters were now in college, thanks to him.

He recently heard the news of Ali's son being kidnapped in Miami. He was crushed when Lil Snoop told him. If it wasn't for Ali, he wouldn't be the man he was today.

One person Butter J was disappointed in was D-Bo, who turned against the crew for a new plug so he could build his own empire. Butter J didn't know the truth of how Joker threatened the lives of the D-Bo family if he didn't trade sides.

Butter J tried to tell D-Bo that Mexicans didn't give a fuck about a nigga from the hood, adding that they would use him and kill him, or give him to the Feds without losing sleep.

The Southside crew was much thicker and solid now with Man-Man holding shit down for the city. With a new connection—an old Dominican cat from Washington Heights—in New York, he was doing good, copping over two thousand dollars every week. Butter J checked his Richard Miller watch worth $1.7 million, realizing Man-Man was late as always.

When he saw the HD lights a block behind in his rear-view, he knew that was Man-Man—plus he heard the hood Mac Dre music blasting a block away. Tonight, the shipment arrived downtown; so he needed Man-Man to bust his weight down with Big Marky.

***

Miami, FL

Ali was moving through the Miami streets in his two-tone black and white Rolls Royce Ghost worth three hundred and seventy thousand dollars, taking up two lanes.

Ali reached out to everybody to help him find his son, but nobody knew anything. This was odd because the city was small, and everybody had ties with everybody.

He hired private investigators, but that was only to use as a backup plan.

Romell Tukes

Being in the game, he knew kidnapping for a ransom was a part of the game; but somebody kidnapped the wrong killer's son.

Ali was looking at bags under his eyes from the lack of sleep. Lately, he'd formed the habit of wearing fuzzy clothes, keeping dirty nails, and he lost a couple of pounds.

The news of Sofia having his daughter shocked him. He disliked Sofia, but he would never disown his own blood.

Seeing the luxury cars speed past him, with the beautiful women and palm trees, kinda brightened his day, as Lil Snoop and his goons were in three SUVs behind him.

He was on his way to have a sit-down with the Cuban Cartel. The only reason he agreed to the meeting was because he wanted to see if Moreno had his son.

He knew Sofia wanted him to shut his casino operation down, but that was out of the question. He refused to shut it down, and he was standing on it.

Ten minutes later, they all pulled up to a small restaurant in Lil Havana to see guards scattered all over the block—on roofs, in windows, on the streets, and in the car parked on the block.

Once inside the restaurant, it was empty as chairs were flipped on top of the table. Moreno sat at a small table, ice-grilling Ali, then changing it to a fake smile.

"Thank you for coming," Moreno said, as he extended his hand to Ali. Frowning, Ali just looked at Moreno's hand and sat down, disrespecting Moreno.

"OK," Moreno said, staring into Ali's dark deadly eyes that made him a little uncomfortable.

"Welcome to Miami, my city. I'm sorry to hear what happened to your family in Vegas, I'm sure Mr. Santana paid with his life for what he did. I heard your son was kid-napped, and I want to clear my face. I don't want to be

38

associated with shit like that. My credibility is high out here and we don't touch kids." Moreno looked at his goons and Ali's goons at the entrance.

"If I have an idea or even a guess you had my son, you'll be dead in that little nice mansion in Shaded Hills under the brown leather pillows you sleep on every night at 12:45."

Moreno's eyebrow raised, and his heart started to race because he slept on a brown leather pillow, and he went to bed every night at 12:45. He was shocked at the accuracy in Ali's statement.

"I understand, Ali, but another reason I asked you to come out here is because of this casino situation. This will bring a lot of issues to us and our turfs. I don't mean to disrespect you, but I must say you are the blacks—so please let me buy you out, then you can just leave before things get out of control." Moneno had a smirk on his face. Ali looked at him as if he lost his mind. He slowly stood up, and Moreno's guards clutched at their weapons.

"Sounds like a war," Ali said.

"If that's what it comes to, Ali—"

"May the best man win!" Ali said.

"I will win—Farewell!" Moreno said. His heart was pounding hard and fast inside of him, but he had a fixed smile on his face to conceal his fear.

Chapter 6

Aguascalientes, Mexico

D-Bo arrived at the large metal gates that were twenty foot high and blocking off the castle-like mansion built from cement in the early 1900's, as guards paced around the property.

D-Bo was in the back seat of the Bentley limousine, fully equipped with laptops, surround sound, flat screen TVs built in the wall, a mini bar, and bullet-proof windows.

The city of Aguascalientes was beautiful, with people flooding the streets selling fruits, water, clothes, jewelry, and anything to feed the poor loved ones.

This was D-Bo's first time visiting Joker. Normally, Spyder would contact him for the pick-ups and drop-offs.

As he exited the limo, he saw men on the rooftop talking through earpieces as six big Mexican guards escorted him inside.

Inside, D-Bo was amazed at the gold chandelier hanging from the fancy painted ceiling. The whole place had a mid-century modern mix of antique classy appeal with modern upgrades.

Walking past the outdoor pool area, D-Bo saw a sign of naked Mexican women with big tits playing in the pool. Enjoying the erotic view of the naked women, his dick got hard while walking toward another section of the 18,919 square foot mansion.

The guard knocked on the double French doors, and a voice shouted for them to enter. D-Bo saw a colossus of cigar smoke in the air, as he walked into an office room with a desk and chairs. The room also had a fireplace, a view of the backyard, with two laptops on Joker's desk.

Joker looked at D-Bo's Michael Kors suit, his bald head and goatee, laughing to himself because to him blacks were like a whore that a man just couldn't turn into a housewife.

"Thanks for the invitation," D-Bo said, sitting in one of the leather chairs.

"No problem, my friend. I hope my G5 jet was comfortable for you," Joker said, blowing smoke in D-Bo's face, before putting his cigar in the ashtray. "You bring me a lot of money, you're a cash cow. I'm glad to have you as a part of my cartel even though you had no choice but a situation as it came up."

D-Bo looked at Joker, wishing he could just whack him because he was a disrespectful racist bastard.

"What's the issue?"

"How about you let me talk and milk this cow while you fuck it! Now as I was saying, I need you and your crew to take care of Ali—which is a part of our deal—and right now is the perfect timing. Ali's son was recently kidnapped." Joker paused, stood up and walked over to his window. "I have no clue who did it, though it was brilliant but very dangerous dealing with a man like Ali. Since he's at his lowest point, I want to make my move. So I expect you to be in Miami within days."

D-Bo was silent. He had no clue Lil Ali was kidnapped. He knew Ali was sick right now. He still had a soft spot for Ali because he never crossed him, and he always showed him love.

"May I also remind you what's at stake here!—I know you love your family, so I'm sure it will be done," Joker said, looking at the women kissing in his pool.

In a sarcastic tone, D-Bo said: "I understand, *master.* Anything else?"

Joker smiled. "No, I know you would always see things my way. Let's enjoy the evening. Those women in the pool are awaiting you. Take the women as a big gift, a token of my appreciation on this month's shipment.

"I'm cool on the women. I have important matters to attend to but I will handle Ali when it's convenient for me. Rest assured the job will get done, bull, and let's make things clear—this is the last time you will threaten my family." D-Bo's tone sounded cold and serious.

"A'ight, but you sure you don't want the women? They're big freaks—unless you're gay or something." Joker laughed as D-Bo stood.

"Nah, I'm good on your flat ass women—I'll be in touch," D-Bo said, walking as he made a mental note of how he'd torture Joker for hours before killing him slowly.

"Big bitch," Joker mumbled under his breath, as he made a mental effort to get rid of D-Bo after Ali was wiped off the face of the earth.

***

Ashkelon, Israel

Jacob had been up since six a.m., taking care of business in both casinos. Since Amina took off from work today, he had to run both casinos.

The traffic was heavy on the tiny expressway today as he drove his black Lotus Evora 400.

Last night, Jacob and Amina went on a nice dinner date on a boat trip he set up, and he proposed to her in front of sixty-something people. Amina thought it was a dream; she screamed *yes* with tears as he gave her a diamond ring worth $7.2 million.

Amina called him earlier when he was in a meeting with Israel's Prince. She told him she had a big surprise for him. She asked him to be inside their condo blindfolded and naked at 10 p.m. while she was out shopping.

When Jacob got home at 9:30 p.m., Amina wasn't there; so he rushed to take a shower, leaving his pistol in the bathroom sink before entering the shower. He was always on alert—thanks to his military training.

As soon as he got out the shower, he placed his gun under his pillow and placed a blindfold on, lying naked on their bed.

Moments later, Amina walked into the house.

"Stay still, baby—just lay back and relax," Amina said, undressing.

"Okay," he said, feeling her hair brush against his bare muscular thighs, as she arranged his legs.

She then placed her soft lips around the end of his massive dick, as he smelled her new perfume. She placed cuffs on his hands, and cuffed him to the bed rails.

Amina swirled her tongue around the crown of his dick, then managed to swallow his entire length deep into her throat, pulling her mouth back up slowly. Her lips were wrapped tightly around his shaft, as he moaned in pleasure.

"Ummmmm—"

She stopped for a second, as Jacob heard another female voice. Amina swallowed his dick again, pumping up and down, violently shaking the bed as she went deeper.

"Oh, shit!" Jacob moaned, wondering where Amina learned that trick from.

She started to take short strokes with long plunges, and she would repeat these moves, taking him down her throat, diving deep on his dick over again, causing him to pump his hips ineffectually at her mouth until he exploded into her throat.

"Mmmmm—" A female moaned, not sounding like Amina, but Jacob didn't say a word.

"Was that good?" Amina said, now pulling the blindfold off his face.

Jacob saw Amina's naked body and a sexy petite Arabian woman with long hair, a cute face and little tits. Like a dream, yet so real, Jacob saw the woman pull Amina close, then she kissed Amina passionately. He was amazed as the Arabian woman licked his cum off Amina's lips. Smiling, Amina placed her pussy in his face, lowering her pussy lips onto his mouth. Jacob opened his mouth readily, taking in the pussy lips and proceeding to give her a wet tonguing that had her moaning like one possessed. "Damn!" Jacob said as Amina climaxed on his face. She turned around so he could eat her ass as the Arabian woman climbed on his dick in the reverse cowgirl. She gasped as his dick went in. This was the largest dick she'd ever taken; she couldn't help but confess that fact. "Ugggg—ohhh—*it's* so big!" the Arabian women yelled, flexing her tight vagina muscles, bouncing up and down.

The fuck fest was all night; they switched into every position and when it was all done, they all went to sleep with big smiles on their faces.

***

Miami, FL

Today was close to 100 degrees outside, and it was the grand opening of the CMA casino which was the talk of Miami. It was the first racetrack/casino/spa/hotel in Miami, so over six hundred people came out to hear Ali give his opening speech in his Armani suit.

When Ali cut the red tape, the crowd went crazy as everybody entered the casino to enjoy themselves.

Everybody came out, the Mayor, rappers, NBA players, gangsters, and his crew. After hours of shaking hands with powerful people, Ali and his crew went to his skyrise office.

The CMA casino had four hundred hotel rooms, a world class spa, a gym, a movie theater, restaurants, clubs, a ball room, a resort, four pools, a horse race track, every gambling machine and table a person would see in Vegas.

"This shit crazy," Lil Snoop said, looking at hundreds of people coming into the casino non-stop.

"You did well, bruh," Haitian Boy said to Ali.

"Yeah, thank you both for helping me out even in my worst moments, but you two help me run the show," Ali said, sitting down.

"Facts but I hollered at every big dawg in the city about Lil Ali and nobody would dare cross that line," Haitian Boy said.

"I'ma leave it to Allah—something will pop up," Ali said.

"We gotta focus on these Cubans also," Lil Snoop said.

"I know them better than I know myself and it's been long past due," Haitian Boy said.

"Their time is coming, let's have a drink and cheers to success," Ali said, pulling out a bottle of expensive champagne and pouring three glasses.

Chapter 7

Miami, FL

Ali was driving back home in the back of his all-white Bentley Mulsanne with tints and custom designed interior insiders. Two Tahoe trucks followed him back to his mansion where his Lil Ali was kidnapped.

The grand opening of the CMA casino was a big hit; he grossed in $7.9 million in one day and was proud of himself.

Ali's driver stopped at a red light, and the street was nearly empty at 11:30 p.m.

When the driver made a sharp left onto the expressway, a car blindsided the Bentley, almost flipping it over as eleven Cubans jumped out with AK-47 assault rifles.

Rat-Tat-Tat-Tat-Tat-Tat-Tat-Tat—

Ali ducked and grabbed his Draco, as glass shattered all over him. His driver was slumped over the steering wheel—dead.

Ali slid out the other side of the Bentley, and started shooting at the barefaced Spanish men as his guards were going round for round.

Ali killed four of them, shooting like a mad man, as well as his guards.

When the Cubans saw it was only two of them left standing, they ran off, dodging bullets as they rushed in the van, racing off.

Ali saw one gunman still trying to crawl to his assault rifle six foot away from him. Ali ran down on the man, kicking him in his side where he'd been shot at twice.

"Ahhhhhh!" the Spanish man screamed in pain, as Ali put his Draco in his face.

"Where is my son?" Ali yelled to the man.

"What kid? We were only sent to kill you," the man cried in pain.

"Who sent you?"

"June, Moreno, and that pretty Puerto Rican phat ass bitch—please get me to a hospital," the Cuban man said in fine English. He looked no older than twenty.

Ali shot him thirteen times in his face, then rushed back to his Bentley, tossing his dead driver on the floor, seeing four of his guards dead. He set the car in motion, and the other five guards followed him on the expressway.

As Ali hit 80 mph down the expressway, he laughed at the attempt on his life. *They just woke up a beast,* he thought.

***

Sparks, Nevada

Fatal was speeding in his new sky-blue Lamborghini Murcielago Roadster. He was on his way home in the suburbs of Nevada, hours outside of Vegas where he and Amber lived together.

Tonight he planned to pop the question because she was the woman he wanted to spend the rest of his life with.

Amber was caring, loving, gentle, loyal, and sexy so he knew the engagement ring worth 3.9 million dollars would make her say *yes*.

He checked his Roger Dubuis Spider Pirelli gold watch, not realizing how late it was as the engine roared through the dark streets.

Fatal heard about Lil Ali being kidnapped and his heart went out to his boss. He asked every powerful boss in Vegas if they had any part in the kidnap, and all of them quickly denied.

48

Pulling into his three-car driveway, he saw an Amber's candy apple green Benz AMG SL 63 roadster coupé parked next to his Wraith, and he had two more parked inside his garage.

The home was a normal two-story brick house with manicured grass, a nice backyard, four bedrooms, two bathrooms, and a fancy living room connected to the dining room.

Their neighbors were an older white couple, who had been married over thirty years, and they talked too much; but most of all, they were nosey.

Mr. and Mrs. Cox were both retired. Mr. Cox was a retired federal judge, and Mrs. Cox was a retired nurse.

As soon as Fatal exited his car, he saw Mrs. Cox peeking out her blinds at him as she did every day. Fatal closed his butterfly doors, shaking his head.

Last week, Mrs. Cox somehow saw him making his Muslim prayer (*salat*) through his bedroom window, and the next day she asked him if he was a terrorist.

"Hey, Mr. Jay," Ms. Cox said, walking outside onto her yard that connects the driveway.

"Hi, it's not past your bedtime?" he said, as she wore a robe exposing her long saggy tits.

"No, it's not but earlier your Muslim friends came to my house looking for you but I directed them to your house. They didn't know your name but I know they was talking about you because you're the only black guy on this block. I believe they were with Amber for a while. They looked scary." Mrs. Cox crossed her arms as the breeze hardened her nipples.

"I'm not understanding—"

"Ask Amber. They were in there for eighteen minutes, thereabouts. I'll see you in the morning, Jay." Mrs. Cox left.

"I hate the Middle Easterners," she said, walking in her home.

Fatal walked into his house, brushing off what Mrs. Cox just said, knowing he was burnt out.

"Amber—Where are you, baby?" he yelled, placing his keys on the hallway table.

As he walked into the living room, he saw boot prints with bloodstains on his white carpet. "Amber!" he yelled, following the blood trail until he made it behind the Fendi couch to see Amber's dead body lying in a puddle of blood in her Chanel lingerie.

"Noooo—nooo—please!" he screamed, seeing her neck was sliced wide open, and she was stabbed over twenty times in her heart.

Fatal dropped down on his knees, holding her dead body in tears, zoned out. When his mind kicked into action, he called Gangsta Ock and told him in code what happened, adding that he was on his way.

Fatal ran upstairs to clean out his safe, and all important documents he had in there also. He was rushing so fast he wouldn't even think straight, but he gathered anything that could to lead this crime scene to him.

Ten minutes later, he rushed into the garage and hopped in this black Wraith.

When he got down the block, he pulled over, crying. Just then, Gangsta Ock texted him, saying he'll be there in thirty minutes with the clean-up crew—so he and the crew were going to make her body disappear, and clean the house of any evidence.

Fatal drove off, wondering why the Muslims looking for him would kill Amber; it didn't add up to him. He didn't even know anybody from the Middle East. He was confused as he was now speeding down the highway with glossy eyes

***

Yazd, Iran

Abu Hurayra was reading the Quran in Arabic in his cabinet house somewhere deep in the Yazd forest surrounded by woods, trees, mountains and the wildlife.

This was a place he would always come to when he needed peace of mind, as his security team surrounded the area 24/7.

Abu Hurayra was the money-hungry type who would turn on anyone for the love of money; so when he went into business with Musa, he knew he was on his way to be a richer man, as he was now—thanks to the casinos.

Abu Hurayra's main source of income was transporting oil through the Persian Gulf and Strait Hormuz maritime pathways. The casino was a gold mine, so he put a plan together to get Ali out of the picture in order to receive 100% profit instead of 50%. Now it was time for Plan C, since plan A and B was already halfway successful.

Abu Hurayra pulled up his private phone and called his most dependable weapon to finish his big plan.

"Hello," a soft voice said, as if she was asleep.

"Hey, princess, daddy needs you to pay Ali a visit, then you can go on vacation somewhere," he told Ayesha who was silent. "Did you hear me?"

"Yes, father, but why did I think—" she said, before he cut her out with a yell.

"I said handle it now—you have one week, no exception," he said, then hung up, pissed off she dared question him.

Chapter 8

Petah Tikva, Israel

Jacob and Amina had a small lovely Islamic wedding at a nice new temple built in the delightful Muslim city of Petah Tikva, known for the biggest mall and shopping outlets in Israel.

"I can't believe we did it, baby, we're finally married," Amina said. "You got me for life now, even an order of protection can't keep us apart." Amina laughed but sounded serious. "Yeah, we're blessed." Jacob said, as they both wore Islamic garments, eating halal food on the rug of the Mosque with other Muslims who were breaking their fast with food for the month of Ramadan.

"We are blessed and we are even more blessed now that I'm pregnant."

"You're what?" he asked, making sure he wasn't hearing shit.

"I'm pregnant," Amina said, smiling as Jacob got hyped, because years ago the doctor told him he may not be able to have kids because his T-Cells were extremely low.

Jacob only wished his father, brother and sister could be here to enjoy the moment. They enjoyed the rest of the evening with the Muslim women and men in the mosque.

***

Miami, FL

Diamond was on Collins Ave, doing some shopping as always.

"Black and gold Versace silk dress will look nice on you," a cute white college girl said, ringing up Diamond's items in the Versace store.

"Thanks," Diamond said, giving her a fake smile while texting Lil Snoop. She wore a sexy two-piece Louis Vuitton midnight blue dress hugging her thick curves and phat ass.

"That will be one hundred and fifty-seven thousand, one hundred and seventy-nine dollars. Would you like to pay in cash or swap?" the clerk asked.

"You asked me the same question before you started to ring my shit up, sweetie. Anyway, I'm paying in cash."

"Diamond, good to see you—is my new worker giving you any trouble?" Jerry—the boss—said, walking towards them in a Versace suit.

"No—she is the best, J," Diamond said, smiling at the white girl, who looked nervous.

"Did you get the purse and belt the company sent? And we also sent that Haitian two Versace custom made suits," Jerry said in his posh voice.

"Yes, we both received it. You're the best. I'll be back next week."

With a smile, Diamond looked at the clerk. "You can keep the change, sweetie," she said to the clerk who was still counting one hundred and sixty thousand dollars' cash Diamond gave her. Jerry snatched all the money out of his worker's hand, yelling something at her as Diamond left the store.

Men eyed her lustfully as she walked down Collins Ave, with six packs in her hands, as she was thinking about her birthday party at Club Live. Haitian Boy's birthday was two days after hers.

Haitian Boy told her he was throwing a lingerie party at his mansion in West Palm Beach, and another in Miami.

Lil Snoop texted her, asking her where she was, and if she wanted to go out to eat dinner.

She loved Lil Snoop to death; he was truly everything she ever wanted in a man, she didn't mind the threesomes because she was bisexual when she wanted to be.

Her ex-boyfriend was a pretty boy nigga who she met in college. He was on his way to being drafted into the NBA. But tragedy struck when he was gunned down in the home of some stripper, who was also found dead alongside the lad. His death left Diamond devastated, until Lil Snoop came into her life and swept her off her feet.

Lil Snoop bought her a pink Porsche Panamera and a pink Benz AMG coupé with custom made interior, big rims, tints, and body kits.

Inside the parking lot, she popped her Benz trunk, pressed the push-to-start button, and tossed the six bags inside the empty trunk. She was itching to get in the car and turn on the A/C because the Miami heat was burning her skin.

When she closed her trunk, she saw a very handsome Puerto Rican nigga standing there wearing a Balmain sweatsuit.

"Hey—How can I help you?" she asked, then she saw him pull out a .44 Bulldog Magnum. Before she could even scream, he shot her twice in her head, then threw her body in the trunk, walking off smoothly.

Neko climbed in the BMW X5, which was full of his Puerto Rican soldiers, pulling off into traffic out the lot.

Neko was a twenty-four-year old Puerto Rican who lived in Miami but was raised in Salinas, PR. He was under the Santana Cartel capo—Rivera—who was Sofia's capo.

Neko controlled the Miami drug trafficking for the family; he had kingpin status. The ladies loved him. He was tall, chiseled, tatted up, long-haired, with green bright eyes, and he stayed dripping in designer clothes.

Sofia was in town, so it was his job to protect his capo with his G-27 gang members who made a big name for themselves in Miami for their vicious murders.

Neko was told there was about to be a big war with Haitian Boy. Ali was against them. Neko was well aware who they were, and there was nothing to be fucked with.

Rivera gave him Diamond's location and told him to whack her. Unaware who she was, Neko followed orders; but for some reason, she looked very familiar, and he could hardly believe how sexy she was before killing her.

***

Ali was staying in his condo on W. South Beach because it didn't feel right at home without Lil Ali there.

The shoot-out with the Cubans had him on point; he was ever ready for war everywhere he went.

Fatal called him earlier, telling him some crazy shit happened and he was on his way to Miami. Ali could tell it was some serious shit from his tone over the phone.

Ali was reading this Noble Qu'ran, trying to maintain a clear state of mind.

***

Miami, FL

Dressed in an all-black tight leather suit, Ayesha slowly crept up Ali's stairwell in his building. She was clutching a H&K mP5 submachine gun that had a silencer and beam attached to it with a 100 shot on a coding system.

Normally, she used knives but she knew Ali traveled with a small army—so she didn't have time to play with her knives today.

Before coming in the building, she hacked into the building's camera system on her laptop, watching how Ali's guards switched positions every hour. She also knew Ali went to sleep at 2 a.m. every morning after praying, and it was 12:30 a.m. now.

There were four guards in the hallway and four guards inside the condo; she saw the guards talking.

"You should have seen Curry," one of them said.

"Man, bruh fragile but when he gets that ball he goes crazy," a man with dreads said.

"I think he is the new Kobe; what do you think?" a tall man with a long beard said.

Before either of the guards could answer, two of them caught headshots, collapsing on the hallway floor.

The other guards looked behind them to see Ayesha duck-walking towards them with a big ass gun.

Psst, Psst, Psst, Psst—She killed the two, and dug in their pockets for the .

The last man had the room key in his back pocket. Ayesha took the key, proceeding to open the door. She slowly walked into the dark condo. She looked around. *His shit is nice*, she thought.

She saw four guards sleeping and snoring loudly on the couch in the living room. She grabbed a leaf off a fresh plant in the corner of the living room.

Ayesha rubbed the thick leaf on one of the men, making him slap himself, then shot him in the head and shot another guard who was sitting knocked out on a love chair.

There were two fat guards left lying next to each other. She slapped one of the men so hard they both woke up, but she'd already ducked behind the couch, laughing under her breath.

"You just slapped me, you bitch ass nigga," the man said, punching the other man. Enraged, the second man stood up with a fresh busted lip, ready to fight—until he saw the other two guards with holes in their head.

Ayesha popped up and shot both men in the face; they both fell back on the couch, going back to sleep for good.

Now it was time to handle business. She sneaked upstairs in the dark condo.

Chapter 9

Ayesha walked into the dark room to see Ali peacefully under his covers in his bed. All types of thoughts were running through her head as she lifted her assault rifle three times, then putting it back down.

"If you're going to kill me, please hurry up," a voice said, coming from behind her, startling her, and she saw Ali's shadow sitting on the floor Indian style. He clapped twice, and the lights came on as she trained her gun on him, knowing he could have killed her.

When he saw it was the same woman who saved his life twice, and the same woman he saw in his dreams, he looked at how sexy she was. He rose, staring at her little camel toe.

The room was silent as they just started at each other. Ali knew someone had been outside watching him for three days, so he acted as if he went to sleep at 2 a.m. but really waiting to see who wanted him dead. He even placed a dummy under his covers, so the gunmen would assume it was him if they made it upstairs.

"I'm sorry—I—I have to do this," she said, fumbling over her word, hesitating to pull the trigger.

"Me too because you can't get out of my mind since the first day I saw you. It's weird because you made me feel something I never felt before, not even for my deceased wife. I'm just glad it's you here to kill me, the woman who I see in my dreams." Ali walked towards her, standing in front of her gun.

She wanted to tell him she felt the same way, and how wet her pussy was, but she was numb and confused. Her mind was racing, and her body was tense.

Ali moved the assault rifle over and kissed her on her soft lips passionately, and she kissed him back. He grabbed her hand, and led her to his bed, pushing the human dummy on the floor, laying her on his Givenchy sheets and pillows.

Ayesha's heart raced as he sucked her hot spot on her neck, then he pulled off her outfit with her help. He saw her bra holding up her perfect breasts, and her pink thong.

When he climbed between her legs, his eyes were greeted by the prettiest pussy he ever saw—small, bold, nice perfect lips, a very small slit, a swollen clit, and pink insides.

He licked her inner thighs, then made his way to her swollen clit and sucked her clit, as her hips ground to the beat of his tongue.

"Ohhhh—" she moaned, gasping for air as she orgasmed within minutes. Her cream leaked everywhere as he fingered her while eating her out.

Ali didn't stop; he continued to hit her G-spot, hitting her highest peak.

"Ohh—I think I'm coming again, ugggh—" she yelled, grabbing a handful of dreads, almost pulling his dreads out as thick warm cum entered his mouth.

"I love you," she said softly, meaning it but shocked at herself for saying it so truthfully.

"I love you too," Ali said honestly, slowly entering her love box. She couldn't even get his tip in as she thrust back.

"Be gentle—please—I never—"

"Shh—" Ali already knew she was a virgin because her pussy was too tight.

Ali worked his way inside of her warm tight pussy, loving every stroke as she moaned loudly, taking deep breaths.

"Damn, you feel good—don't stop, never—please," she said, feeling pain and pleasure as spasms shot through her pussy. While he pushed in and out, as she wrapped her toned legs around his waist, making him go deeper as he relaxed her pussy muscles.

Ali was now fucking her so good he was about to cum.

"Uggghhh—yessss—dammmm!" she groaned louder. The slippery sound of their sweat-soaked clapping bodies could be heard as they both hit their climax.

He bent her over to see her pussy and that perfect gap between her legs. He grabbed her lovely round ass and smacked it as she put her ass up, and face down into the pillows.

Ali started to fuck her slowly, feeling her bottom as her pussy muscles grabbed his dick with every long stroke, as she went bananas.

"Oh, my god! Fuck me—Ohhhhh—" she yelled as he thrust his hips onto her ass cheeks, giving her the entire pipe until they both climaxed again.

Ali saw small blood stains, as she finally pulled out her open pussy.

"Oh no! I'm sorry," she said, covering her mouth when she saw her blood because she finally lost her virginity.

"I got it."

"No, I got it."

"No, Ayesha, I do. Go take a shower, but did you mean what you said?"

"How do you know my name? And yes, I meant every word of it, did you?"

"Yes," he said, passing her a silk Gucci robe. She went to take a shower, feeling like a new woman. She couldn't believe what just happened, as she was so happy she was on the verge of screaming.

Ali went downstairs to yell at his guards, wondering how they let her inside to kill him. When he saw all the dead guards in the living room and hallways, he called team B to clean the mess up. He was a little upset because he hated losing men.

***

Acapulco, Mexico

Joker and Spyder arrived at Ole Bay's beach glass house surrounded by white sand behind a riverfront.

Ole Bay personally called Joker to a meeting which made him a little nervous because Ole Bay had the biggest, most violent Cartel family in Mexico, and he was an ally with the Peru Cartel—the biggest Cartel family in the world

Joker entered the home to see eighty-something guards everywhere staring at him and Spyder as they left their twenty-five guards outside.

Ole Bay ran the Gomeze Cartel. His father was 100% Mexican; his mother was a black Dominican woman from Philly. When his father died, he left Ole Bay his empire.

He was born and raised in North Philly with his mother, an RN nurse who was very beautiful. She met his father on a vacation in Mexico and got pregnant. When she informed him, he told her about his lifestyle, and they made an agreement to keep a distance from each other—for the child's safety.

Ole Bay was a part of the black Mafia, which was comprised of him, Musa, Big Ali, Akbar, and Havoc. They were all family, and he was the only Mexican nigga in South Philly at the time killing shit. When his father died, he was left to take over his father's empire after he was kidnapped by Mexicans loyal to his father, and they brought him to Mexico where they told him he was the new boss.

Ole Bay was in his conference room with his capo— Big Loco—who was a big master fresh home from doing twenty years in prison; he was one of the deadliest niggas in

Mexico. Big Loco ran an army of killers who killed kids, grandmoms, judges, cops, and whoever got in their way.

"Our guest is here," Big Loco said in Spanish as Joker and Spyder walked in the room while Ole Bay looked at them.

Ole Bay was short, golden-complexioned, fit, and long-haired. He had a goatee, thick earlobes, no grays, and he was a smooth talker.

"Good to see you both," Joker said in Spanish as he was about to sit.

"No need to sit," Ole Bay began, looking at Joker with a frown. "This will be quick. I got wind that you have issues with a kid named Ali."

"Looks like he's the boss," Big Loco said with a chuckle, pointing at Joker.

"I need you to leave him alone and this is my only warning—if one hair is touched on him, your whole family will regret," Ole Bay said sternly.

"I understand," Joker said, holding his anger, wondering how Ole Bay even knew about the low life street punk.

"Good, now get the fuck out," Big Loco stated for his boss, not liking Joker at all.

Joker left the mansion, deciding he'd refuse to let Ole Bay come between his plans, or he would kill him.

***

Miami, FL

Fatal rode in the Benz limo on his way to pay Ali a visit to explain everything that's been going on. He left Gorilla in charge of the casino because he knew the business operations.

Fatal put everything together, and he only came up with one conclusion—that it was Abu Hurayra who sent his men to kill him. *But for what reason*? Fatal wondered, hoping Ali could put the missing pieces of the puzzle together for him.

Driving through Miami, he saw flamingos and hawks flying around; beautiful Latin women in bikinis; palm and pine trees everywhere.

Fatal was going through an emotional phase every second. First, it was Brittany and his daughter—Kelly; now it was Amber. He felt as if he was cursed.

He swore he would kill everyone Abu Hurayra ever loved or even cared for.

Chapter 10

Miami, FL

Ali spent a whole day cleaning the blood trail Ayesha left in his condo and hallway. He felt lucky he had a whole floor to himself with no neighbors.

There was blood all over his mink rugs. He had to have a cleaning service come in to clean, then he had Lil Snoop get rid of the bodies.

Ayesha hadn't left his side since the other night. He had his guards buy her whatever she wanted. They knew she was the woman who killed their co-workers because Ali told them, just so they could be on point if she played two sides.

Ali never felt this way about a woman, not even Sofia or Laura; he grew to love them, but with Ayesha the love came natural. He questioned her about her mission to kill him, and she told him the truth.

When he asked her about his son, she told him she knew nothing about his kid being kidnapped, and she told him her father didn't touch kids or civilians; if he wanted a person dead, then he would go straight for them

She told him she was on his side now, and was willing to help even though she was already a dead bitch walking.

Years ago, as a teenager, she took an oath because she was forced to. The oath bound her to complete every mission her father sent her on; and if not, she will be murdered. When she told Ali this, he was surprised a person could treat their own children so cruel.

Ali was sitting on another couch in a Nike sweatsuit, drinking tea, reading '*48 Laws of Power*', trying to map out a plan to find out who kidnapped Lil Ali, and how he was going to get him back.

He still didn't trust Ayesha, but she was a good figure to have on his team. She was sleeping from the long night of sex.

"Boss, excuse me, Fatal is here," one of his guards said, walking in the condo with Fatal behind him.

"Damn, you got a hundred guards out there," Fatal said, walking in with his screw face.

"Fatal, what's good, cuz?" Ali said, embracing him.

"They killed Amber, they stabbed her to death. They were desert niggas."

"What? Slow down, Fatal, how do you know it was them?"

"My neighbors saw them Arabian niggas. The only Middle Eastern connects we have is that Abu Hurayra character. I'm telling you, it was them." Fatal walked across Ali's living room floor.

"Damn! I'm sorry, man, I'm getting to the bottom line of this," Ali replied. As Fatal was about to say something, he saw the sexy foreign woman in a Prada robe, as she walked in the kitchen.

"Who is that?" Fatal asked.

"Ayesha—she's Abu Hurayra's daughter. She's—" Before Ali could even finish his sentence, Fatal pulled out his gun, running down on Ayesha. "Fatal, chill out!" Ali yelled.

Ayesha sidestepped Fatal and grabbed his pistol so fast he didn't even see it as she reversed the floor and then she released the last bullet in the chamber.

That shit happened so fast both men were shocked. And Ali walked Fatal into the living room, and sat him down before he himself took a seat. Ayesha approached them. "I swear to Allah, I had nothing to do with the death of your loved ones. If I did, then you wouldn't be here right now. If you want to kill, please be my pleasure," she said, crossing her legs. She'd been asleep until she heard Fatal's loud talk, and she crawled out to check on her boo.

"Fatal, just listen—she is with me, bro, I need her to trust me."

"You fucking this bitch, you don't see what's going on—she's setting you up—she's going to vanquish you at your weak point," Fatal said, picking up his gun clip.

"Calm down, we need her point."

"So you trust her?"

"For now yes. It's not about us, Fatal, it's about us finding out who killed your family and who kidnapped my son. We're stronger together than apart," Ali said.

"You're sleeping with the enemy so your mind state is blinded by pussy, nigga, she going to stab you in your back with a knife and turn it."

"She is worth the risk and I'm standing on it."

"Since you choose her side, you ride with her, you die with her," Fatal said, rushing out the crib, staring at Ayesha as she stared back showing no fear.

"Fuck!" Ali yelled, knocking over all the pots and pans on his countertop. Ayesha walked over to him, hugging him from behind.

"I'll never turn on you—not even in my casket."

"I hope not," he said, turning to kiss her soft lips, seeing how sexy she was without make-up.

Ali felt as if he was making the right choice with Ayesha; he only wished Fatal could see shit his way. Now he was another friend turned enemy.

***

South Philly

Man-Man was driving in his new pearl white 1970 Oldsmobile 422 convertible with gold stripes and Louis Vuitton interior. The car had 26-inch big Asanti Black label rims.

He was driving through the hood to pick up some money with Dream who was the baddest bitch in Philly.

She was a redbone, with long fake blonde hair, tattoos, and green eyes. She was thick with 36-30-40 measures.

Dream just lifted her head out his lap from sucking his dick; he'd cum in her mouth three times in the last hour.

"Baby, can we get something to eat after you pick up your money?" she asked, as he drove through 14th to see niggas out trapping as he rode through the streets with his top back.

"Bitch what the fuck I look like? A meal ticket? Matter of fact, get your dry pussy ass the fuck out, McDonalds up the street, bitch!" Man-Man said, pulling over to the curb, pushing her onto the curb and tossing her fake Birkin bag—which read: *Made in China*—at her.

"I'm sorry—You're gonna make me walk home out here?" she said, standing up, fixing her dress and wig.

"Nah, bitch, call an Uber if you find some Wi-Fi service out here," he said, pulling off, laughing and turning up the YG and Nipsey song in his system.

Man-Man stopped at a red light and texted his homie—Chris—letting him know he was a block away, so he'd better be ready.

South Philly had been hot lately because a cop was shot in the head on duty last week, so Philly PD had been harassing everybody.

As soon as he was about to pull off, he saw a familiar face at the Exxon gas station across from him hopping out a yellow Porsche Panamera.

"Bitch ass nigga!" he muttered under his breath, pulling over at the sight of D-Bo. He looked closer and saw Pacman in the passenger side of D-Bo's car.

D-Bo just got done pumping gas, and he walked into the convenience store to purchase some snacks because he had the munchies after smoking a half ounce of sour. Pacman joined him in the store. "Bruh, I don't have much dough on me—Mind getting me some cookies?" Pacman said.

"No probs, man," D-Bo said. He was in Philly to visit his beautiful sister and parents in their house in the suburbs of Philly before he went to Miami. He'd been driving down towards the gas station when he saw Pacman standing by the roadside. He'd pulled over right away; and after they exchanged pleasantries, Pacman told him he was going to Miami to see his baby mama. D-Bo told him to hop in, since he himself would be going that way soon.

After D-Bo paid for his gas, a box of Dutches, an Arizona Ice Tea, a bag of Doritos, and a pack of Pepperridge Farm cookies, he waited for his change. Pacman stepped outside after D-Bo handed him the cookies. He ripped the pack open, his head lowered, as he focused on eating the cookies instantly.

"Pacman—" D-Bo yelled.

Pacman looked back, and saw D-Bo rushing out of the store. "Look out!" D-Bo screamed. It was too late for Pacman, as four bullets landed in his chest, sending him stumbling backwards into the store, the cookies falling from his hands.

Boom, Boom, Boom, Boom, Boom—D-Bo fired at Man-Man, as he took cover because Man-Man's Draco was overpowering his 9mm Glock.

Man-Man shot out his windows and mirrors, trying to take his head off, but D-Bo hopped up shooting as he ran for his driver side door, then he noticed he was out of bullets. Pedestrians ran everywhere down dirty alleys, into crack houses, or in buildings, trying not to get hit.

"Don't hide, bruh!" Man-Man yelled, shooting D-Bo's passenger door side.

D-Bo was able to hop in his Porsche. He raced off as Man-man chased the Porsche out the gas station, letting off shots from his Draco.

Man-Man heard sirens, which made him run down an alley and jump over two gates with ease, leading to another block where he tossed the Draco in the dumpster.

Once on Jefferson St, he walked past a young crew of goons smoking weed with Dream who was sitting on the steps waiting for the eight niggas to pass one blunt.

When he walked past, they treated him like God, hailing him as Dream kept her head down with a dumb look on her face as if she already fucked the whole crew.

Man-Man made it to 13th street on foot, and he called Big Marky to pick up his car and the money from Chris. As he went to his apartment to prepare for the night, he texted Dream, telling her to pull up. She texted back, saying she'll be there in five minutes.

Chapter 11

Daytona Beach, FL

"Oh, yesss, papi, me like that," Karen moaned wildly while Moreno devoured her hard brown nipples that were in the center of her large areolae.

Karen was 100% Cuban and the Latina model type—tall, with long and sleek jet-black hair, nice firm ass, brown eyes, pretty edges, a cute smile, and a sexy walk.

She was Moreno's stepdaughter. At nineteen, she fucked like she was forty. She loved older men, and they loved her shallow tight wetness.

Moreno's wife was in Paris shopping; so when the cat's away, the mice always came out to play as usual. Moreno loved when his wife went out on vacations.

Karen was once pregnant by him, but he made her get an abortion which she was mad about. She hated her mother; that was one reason she loved to fuck him crazy.

Moreno ate her nice little Brazilian wax pussy, as she whimpered while her legs quivered with every delicate touch of his tongue, while he fingered her.

Karen fucked his finger until her body tightened and went rigid,

"Fuck me, pop," she moaned in her strong Spanish accent as he entered her, rubbing the bulbous head of his dick up and down in her dripping wet slit covering his dick with her juices, before he started to fuck her slowly.

'Uggghhh—papi, yesss—" She gritted as he thrust in and out until she quickly climaxed.

"I want to suck it, put it in my mouth," she begged, opening her mouth greedily, sucking his dick while moaning around his shaft, making slurping sounds.

She sucked him so good he held on to her head, as she slid her thin lips rapidly up and down on his average-size tan-colored dick. She gobbled him up until he came in her mouth and all over her face. She wished her mom could see her with her husband's cum all over her face.

"You're amazing, baby—now clean up, your mom should be home today," he said, as she stood up and put on a robe.

He loved fucking her young pussy; he knew it was bad parenting, but she wasn't his daughter. Moreno called June to speak to him about the big situation at hand.

***

Lil Havana, Miami

Haitian Boy couldn't get the vision of his little sister lying dead in a casket out of his head. He knew who was responsible for the hit—the Cubans or Puerto Ricans—and he vowed to kill as many of them as possible.

Lil Snoop was crushed when he got the call his wifey was dead. He became another person, and he wanted answers, but through blood.

Lil Havana was where all the Cubans resided in Miami; it was a lower class ghetto that looked like Cuba.

June and Moreno controlled the section they ran which was characterized by residential houses, gambling, sports, dope houses, and weapon trafficking, as well as big prostitution rings. Tonight, Haitian Boy and Lil Snoop put their plan in full effect as they both laid back in an old Honda with tints in the middle of the block.

"Is everybody in place?" Haitian Boy asked on his walkie-talkie, tying his long palm tree dreads in a ponytail.

There was a crew on every section of the block, inside cars, behind buildings, under dumpsters, in the kitchen.

Haitian Boy was now upstairs in a vicious gun battle against six niggas and four bitches that were taking out his men back to back.

Tat-Tat-Tat-Tat-Tat-Tat—Haitian Boy shot the door frame, but hit two of the bitches as five of his men ambushed the room, killing everything in it.

Haitian Boy ran in the bathroom, shooting, gunning down two fat Cuban men trying to hide in the tube.

The gunfire downstairs was sounding like Pearl Harbor in World War II.

Lil Snoop dived as eight bullets flew past his face; he saw three dead Haitians within two feet of him.

"Bitch—" Lil Snoop ducked as eight bullets flew past his face, he saw three dead Haitians within two fcct of him.

"Bitch!" Lil Snoop yelled, as three bitches were in the small old-fashioned living room letting off shotguns. When he saw Haitian Boy come down stairs, he directed him to the other entrance of the living room so he could distract them.

When he saw the naked big-breasted women were focused on Haitian Boy and his crew, he crept up on them, shooting all of them in their pretty faces.

The Haitians cleaned out the house, scoping out the abandoned building across the street from the main targeted location.

"Yeah, bro, everything is a go—we see five Cubans outside and a lot of movement in the yellow house," one of the shooters replied over the walkie-talkie, watching the scene on the dark block with a dead end.

"You ready?" Haitian Boy asked Lil Snoop, who stood somberly to the right of him, dressed in a black Dickie suit with a M-16 rifle in his lap as Haitian Boy grabbed the AK-47 with a shoulder strap and banana clip.

"Let's do it," Lil Snoop said flatly.

"Go, go, go!" Haitian Boy yelled through his walkie-talkie to see niggas coming from everywhere, bum-rushing the yellow house where the Cubans were.

Haitian Boy and Lil Snoop ran into mayhem as the Haitian killed the five guards outside, not even giving them a chance to grab their weapons.

The crew kicked in the door to see gunfire from naked Spanish women shooting rifles and handguns while running around.

"Split up!" Lil Snoop yelled, taking out two Cuban men shooting from behind a money machine. Once they stepped outside, it was more mayhem as Cubans came out of houses, shooting toward the crew.

"Cover me!" Haitian Boy yelled to Lil Snoop, hitting every target as the Cubans kept coming while most of the Haitians ran back in the houses because they were of ammo.

Haitian Boy climbed on top of the roof of an old-school Cutlass supreme, and reloaded as Lil Snoop killed two Cubans sneaking from behind a brick building while seven more were scattered around the block.

Haitian Boy lit up the block like Christmas lights in a rich gated neighborhood. He looked like a madman, shooting everything in sight, and Lil Snoop had to duck.

A police cruiser pulled on to the block. The lone police officer in the cruiser was from Miami PD, and when he saw Haitian Boy on top of the car shooting up the block, as bodies were dripping back to back, he reversed and got the fuck out of there, remembering it wasn't his beat time anyway.

Two minutes, later the block was smoky with the smell of gunpowder. There were only four men left standing outta the twenty-six Lil Snoop came with, as they all left with blood on their hands.

"You're hungry?" Haitian Boy asked Lil Snoop.

"I can do for some waffle house."

"Huh—we out, bruh."

***

Jerusalem, Israel

Jacob rode in his white, red and black Pagani Huayra coupé sports car with Amina in the passenger seat texting her family the good news that she was having a baby girl.

Lately, Jacob hadn't heard from Ali; he would normally call monthly to check on him and the casinos, so he found that a little odd, but he planned to call him tonight.

Jerusalem had the best doctors in Israel, and it was the biggest city in Israel. It was very beautiful and clean, unlike certain parts of Israel,

"What do you want to name her, baby?" she asked, as he was driving over a small bridge.

"Whatever you find suitable, baby, but *Laura* would be nice," he replied, recalling the name of his sister who was killed.

"That's perfect, baby," she said, holding his hand on the way home from her doctor appointment. Thinking about his unborn child, Jacob was unaware of the two old Benz wagons tailing him.

"Can you believe my parents are still salty that I am Muslim? They believe in our tribal culture and religion;

anything else is considered an anomaly to them. Can you imagine—" *Bloc, Bloc, Bloc, Bloc!*

"Get down!" Jacob yelled, as bullets entered the passenger door, and he quickly pulled out a chrome 300 Winchester magnum, shooting out his window, hitting the Benz driver in his neck. While his focus was on the Benz on his right, whose driver he just shot, he was unaware of the Benz on his left; the vehicle rammed his car, almost crashing him into a cab.

"Shit!" Jacob said, bopping through traffic as he looked over to Amina. "Baby, wake up, Amina—" he yelled, as he saw blood leaking from her upper torso and her stomach. "Hold on—" Jacob said, as the Benz wasn't letting up. Jacob shot out his the back window of his own car, and the window shattered to pieces, giving him leeway to fire at his assailant.

Jacob slowed down so he could get a look at the driver who was now coming close up. He recognized the assailant there and then. It was Isaac—Abu Hurayra's son. He was coming closer. Jacob fired two shots out his window; the bullets pierced through the windscreen of the Benz, hitting Isaac twice in the head.

Isaac's car crashed into two large full water containers, as Jacob got off the exit to see a hospital. He hoped Amina was still alive, as he raced to the entrance that had big Arabic signs.

Jacob carried her inside, yelling as two Arabian doctors came out and told him to follow them.

Once in the trauma unit, the doctors tried to shake her back to life to get a pulse.

Jacob was in the lobby, trying to hold it together. He couldn't figure out why Abu Hurayra's son would try to kill him. He and Isaac worked together with the casino, and they were always cool initially.

"Sir, I'm sorry—she was dead before she came through the door; we tried everything—I'm sorry," the doctor said, trying not to look at Jacob's face. "She also lost the baby. Sorry, sir."

Jacob turned and left with tears of pain and hurt in this heart.

***

Miami, FL

Butter J had only been in Miami for three hours, and he was in a red Lambo Aventador. Lil Snoop was behind him in a white Ferrari 488 GTB coupé on their way to Carol City because Butter J had a chick out here named Ashley. He was in town to spend time with the boys and enjoy a vacation.

Chapter 12

Miami, FL

West South Beach had one of the hottest clubs in the city—Club Storm. The club had two levels, two stages for performers, a pool in the back area, and for large VIP sections. Tonight the club was live, loaded with elegantly dressed beautiful women, ballers rocking big diamond chains and big-face Rolexes; everybody was out for a good time and a nightcap

"Damn, this spot popping," Butter J said in his all-red Versace outfit with a colorful lion on his shirt and pants.

"This is my everyday life," Lil Snoop replied, and yelled for a beautiful bottle girl to keep the bottle of Ace and D'usse coming.

The two were in the VIP section, enjoying the scene as Lil Snoop looked like money in his white and gold Louis Vuitton outfit with a gold Cuban chain and a gold Rolex watch.

"You been down here so long you back like a country nigga," Butter J said, pouring himself a cup of Ace, looking at Lil Snoop's dreads. "You even starting to sound like these niggas.

"I just copped a 1974 Impala worth thirty something thousand—I put it in a car show too they are having on South Beach," Lil Snoop said.

"That's what's up, cuz, I may need to get a crib out here. Philly is getting worse again."

"I heard but I wish you could meet wifey," Lil Snoop said, sadly looking at his goons in the other VIP section next door to them, with a gang of bitches dancing on couches to a *Rich the Kid* song.

"It's cool, bro, that's life, bro," Butter J said. "We gotta take the good with the bad but you came a long way and so did Ali. Y'all took Philly to a whole 'nother level. Now everybody want to be a boss."

"Facts."

"Your boy Man-Man had a shoot-out with this fuck boy D-Bo. He got his man, but D-Bo got away."

"Fuck that double cross nigga, but Man-Man a wild boy," Lil Snoop said, as he saw the familiar face walk in the club. "We got issues—" Lil Snoop watched Neko's every move, and Butter J looked towards Neko's direction.

Neko entered the club with ten goons. The whole club embraced him in his green Gucci suit as if he was Uncle Luke.

Neko was half drunk already; this was the third club for the night he attended as he mingled with hustlers, the kingpins, and beautiful women.

The only thing on his mind was Sofia; yesterday, he met her at her South Beach condo for a meeting.

When she saw he couldn't keep his eyes off her body, she told him if he likes his eyes, then he would keep them in his sockets before they disappeared with his body and soul.

Then she added that black men were her sexual preference, not controlling Spanish men; but Neko still wanted every inch of her, even though she was his boss.

Neko pulled out his phone. Still drunk, he texted Sofia. He stated in the text that she was beautiful and he wanted to taste her. He placed his phone in his pocket, hoping she texted back as he bobbed his head to the Migos' song.

"I'ma go piss," he told one of his goons talking to a thick Cuban woman.

"A'ight," the tall man said, paying his boss no mind as he thought about how good the bitch's pussy was going to be in front of him. Neko walked through the cross to the bathroom in the corner of the club. He entered the clean bathroom and took a piss for two minutes straight, releasing all the clear liquor he was sipping.

Without a sign in his hands, he walked out the bathroom to see a pistol pointed in his face in the dark blind spot area.

"Whoa! What is this about" Neko asked with his hands up, looking at the crew of dread heads. "My people have no issues with Jamaicans," he said, getting the group of Haitians mad. Lil Snoop chuckled.

"You killed the woman in the parking lot?" Lil Snoop asked, as Neko's face tended to give him away.

"I work for Rivera who works for Sofia—I don't know anything else," he said, as two black women who'd been taking a shit came out of the lady's restroom. When they saw the crazy Haitians with guns raised, they rushed out of the rest room, knowing full well that Haitians from Dade County loved to shoot up clubs.

"Did you kill her?" Lil Snoop yelled, shoving the P89 Ruger in his mouth, and kicked out a front tooth as Neko wanted to cry.

Neko nodded and Lil Snoop blew his brain all over the men's bathroom door, then all hell broke loose with the Haitians and G27 gang.

Bullets were flying everywhere as party-goers were running all around, dodging bullets.

Within minutes, six Haitians were dead; eight G27 niggas and four civilians were caught in the cross fire.

When police arrived, two G27 and five Haitians were arrested and taken to Dade County Jail. Luckily for Lil Snoop and Butter J, they sneaked out the back exit leading to their vehicles.

***

Ali just received an envelope full of photos of Lil Ali's arms and legs covered in dirt. The horrendous sight brought tears to his eyes.

When Ayesha saw the photos, she noticed something was off and awkward about the whole scene; however, she kept it to herself, as Ali was venting. She knew Lil Ali was already dead.

Chapter 13

Yazd, Iran

Abu Hurayra stood over his fireplace in his living room, looking at the pictures of his son who was killed months ago.

He was speaking to his son—Israel—who was sitting, listening. "I don't understand how this could happen to him. He was well-trained, yet he let an ex-marine kill him. This was supposed to be easy but you all are making this shit very hard. Your sister is nowhere to be found. I wasn't going to bury her next to Issac."

'I understand, father," Israel said.

"I want you to find the little bitch. She could fuck up everything."

"We already have our people in Miami on the hunt for her," Israel said, standing to leave as his soldiers waited for him outside.

Once he was gone, Abu Hurayra walked downstairs into his basement which was large with two rooms, a living room, kitchen, and a bar.

One room was med-size, sound-proof, with a twin-size bed, TV, Xbox game system, and toys everywhere behind the fiber glass windows.

Lil Ali was behind the fiberglass, eating mini Oreo cookies with milk.

Abu Hurayra was behind Lil Ali's kidnap; it was all a part of his plan to divide and conquer to get to the top.

The pictures he recently sent Ali were to only weaken his mind and thought process, so he can run circles around him.

Lil Ali was playing "Call of Duty" on the Xbox game system and felt someone stare at him, but that was normal to him now. There were guards in the basement 24/7 watching him, but Lil Ali knew what was going on,

He missed his father and his home. The first chance he got, he swore to run away as far as possible. Even though they treated him decently, he wanted to go home.

***

Miami, FL

D-Bo just got comfortable in his nice hotel suite in the new hotel called the CMA. Someone at the airport told him about it, and he was amazed the place was top-notch.

He was here for one mission—to kill Ali and get back to his paper chase.

Every day he was thinking about what happened with him and Man-Man. He vowed after this Ali situation to kill Man-Man. He never came so close to losing his life as he did recently, which is why he had to get rid of Man-Man asap.

Joker had a crew situated in Miami for D-Bo. He'd placed the crew under D-Bo's command to supply him with weapons and shooters.

***

North Miami

Sofia was in a classy spa with a green facial mask on her face, getting her feet and nails done.

Since she'd been in Miami, nothing had worked out in her favor. She thought speaking to Ali would change his mind about his casino that was now the talk of Miami.

She had been pushing buttons on Ali's life. However, for some reason, her people kept coming back in body bags.

The city had been a war zone since the killing of Neko. *Whoever this Haitian Boy is, he is really putting on for Ali's camp,* Sofia thought.

Two weeks ago she sent her daughter to Puerto Rico to live with her Godmother just until the fire died down because—she had to admit—Ali was going mad.

Sofia was going to kill Neko anyway, after he did all the dirty work and showed disrespect through the text he sent her.

One of her guards handed her a phone. She checked the phone and saw a text from Rivera saying he just landed in Miami and he would be seeing her soon.

***

Key West, FL

Ali and Ayesha were on his yacht. She was on the lower deck, and the sun hit her bikini lines as she showed her sexy, toned shapely body.

Ali wore Polo shorts in the bedroom, calling Jacob but only getting voicemail. With everything going on, he forgot all about Jacob in Israel.

"You're okay, bae?" Ayesha yelled as Ali came upstairs and joined her. Every time he saw her beautiful face, his heart warmed up.

"I'm good," he said, slapping her nice round ass. She giggled. "I got a question, baby, if it comes down to it would you kill your family for me?" Ali asked because he had a feeling Abu Hurayra was up to no good.

"Yes, I will, baby, I can never love a person I don't know or trust. My dad hired someone to kill my mom years ago and made it look like some sort of retaliation but when I found the man that murdered my mom, he confirmed my father paid him," she said sadly looking into his eyes.

"Damn, wow! I know this is an awkward time, Ayesha, but I fell head over heels for you, and I want to spend the rest of my life with you. When I first laid eyes on you, I knew you were the one. So with all that being said, will you marry me?" Ali asked, popping the question.

"Wha—are you serious? Oh, my god!" she screamed her voice echoing through the ocean. "Yes, I will love to," she said, kissing him, and one thing led to another.

She grabbed his penis and pulled it out his shorts, placing her lips on his hard pole, as she slowly sucked it up and down on his base, while massaging his balls, trying to deep-throat him.

After he came, she swallowed it all and climbed on his dick, riding it as she felt him in her insides, bouncing up and down until they both climaxed.

The two fucked all evening and night.

Chapter 14

Miami, FL

Rivera sat in the fancy restaurant on Collins Ave, waiting for Sofia who was late as always. He hated coming to Miami because he had a fifteen-year warrant for murder, and he wasn't trying to go to jail; life was too sweet.

He was forty-five years old but looked thirtyish because he took good care of himself. Most people thought he was Crazy Legs from the Rock Steady Crew because they looked like twins, and he was from his hood—Isabela, PR

Sofia finally walked in the restaurant with her goons. She wore a white Dolce and Gabbana V-neck dress showing her large breasts and upper abs.

Customers stared at her crazy body as if she was a video vixen in front of their wives who cussed their husbands out.

"Hey Mr. Evilface," she said, laying her Birkin bag on the table.

"Next time can you fucking come on time and decently dressed?" Rivera said, watching people watch her.

She took of her Bottega Veneta shades. "I'm a grown woman. I can dress how I please. It's not my fault men can't keep their little dicks in their pants."

"I already ordered for us because I knew you would be late."

"Sorry about that but let me update you on what's been going on. Neko was killed by Ali's people."

"You got a name and address yet?"

"Leave Ali for me but you can take care of them Jamaicans or Haitians—whatever—they are Lil Snoop and Haitian Boy."

"Haitian Boy? Damn it! That's a hard fucker to kill but I'll get it done. Are you sure you can handle Ali? I hear he is very dangerous."

"Did you hear what the fuck I just said? I will handle him!" Sofia never told anyone Ali was the child's father except Ali himself.

"I understand, boss."

"Good, now where is my food? I hope it's your treat.

"Not at all, love."

"This is how you treat a lady?" she said as their food finally arrived.

***

Key West, FL

Ali and Ayesha just got married in a small mosque in North Miami. He found her a nice ring at 13.2 million dollars, filled with VVS diamond he had shipped from Africa.

"I don't want a honeymoon, baby, at least not right now—I got a lot going on," she said, as they were in the back of his Maybach, with bullet-proof Callaway Tahoe trucks tailing them.

Ayesha was in an all-white Alexandra Bouttier Couture dress while Ali wore a black tuxedo, looking like a don.

"I'm down for whatever, but I have a big surprise," Ali said as the Maybach entered the gated community full of beautiful mansions.

Ayesha was at a loss for words when she saw the lushly landscaped surroundings. "Oh, my god! Baby, this is beautiful," she said, as they got out of the car to see the large magnificent stone mansion with glass front doors.

"Come in, check out your new home," Ali said, holding her hand as they walked inside on the marble heated floors to a 40 ft. vaulted ceiling.

The mansion had ten bedrooms, seven bathrooms, a large living room, a wood panel library, a water aquarium, a movie theater, walk-in closets, walk-in pantries, three floor levels, a large backyard with a large pond and a mid-size pool connected to it. The mansion was 24,712 square feet and on 13 acres of land. The mansion had been placed at 23.5 million dollars, but Ali got it for 21.4 million dollars after a conscientious bargain.

"Your Wraith and Aston Martin should be here in the morning," he said, as she jumped in his arms, and he felt two handguns under her dress as he kissed her, loving every second of their intimacy.

***

Overtown, Miami

Haitian Boy just switched his old-school car for his Ferrari 488 Spider. He pulled out his apartment parking lot, as a car full of Haitians waited in a '96 Impala across the street for their boss and best friend.

Lately, Haitian Boy had been hunting down June and Moreno because he knew all their war tactics from their previous war.

Once he got on the highway, he turned up the Kodak Black album.

A blue Jeep cut him off, almost making him hit another truck on the side of him as he blew his horn. Haitian Boy looked to his left to see an AK 47 with a drum attached to it trying to get a good aim.

"Shittttt! Puerto Ricans!" Haitian Boy ducked and speeded up as the Jeep in front stopped, blocking him in as the AK 47 tore through his passenger door, hitting him twice as he swerved into the next line; then the Puerto Ricans raced out.

A black Escalade truck savagely slammed into the Jeep, then shooters sprayed Draco bullets at the Jeep, making it swerve into the opposite lane where it crashed into a lamp post and exploded on impact. Haitian Boy was feeling weak as his goons finally caught up with him. Then, out of nowhere, the black Escalade fired shots into the Impala, killing two of the Haitians as they slammed into the wall.

Haitian Boy saw the gunman aiming his Draco at him, but he raced off the Liberty City exit, trying to get to Ella's house.

Ella was a nurse and his side bitch. She lived a block around the corner from the highway. She was his only choice as blood soaked his Gucci shirt. He was trying to stay awake.

***

Chihuahua, Mexico

Ole Bay reached Ali days ago to set up a sit-down in Texas so they could meet halfway on fair grounds.

Ole Bay didn't know why Joker wanted Ali dead. He dermined to make sure that never happened on his watch. Ali's late dad—Big Ali—was the man that always had Ole Bay's back and showed him love since middle school when he had to fight black kids every day to prove he was just as tough as them.

Ali's name was ringing for years especially after how he ran out or killed all the Mob bosses in Vegas and in the Tri-State area.

***

El Paso, Tx

Ali walked into the empty Mexican restaurant alone, leaving his guards outside.

Ole Bay was sitting alone at a table, drinking rum and coke.

"Ali, welcome," Ole Bay said, shaking his hand. "You look just like your father. Have a seat."

"Who are you?—No disrespect as regards my question, please," Ali said to the man who looked like a ghetto Mexican with black people swag.

"I am getting straight to the point. I run the biggest Cartel family in North and South America. I was raised in Philly—your father and I were close. I was down with the Black Mafia."

"Oh, you're Ole Bay. I heard of you. Musa talked about you once before."

"Good Ole Musa—may he rest in peace. He was a good man. Anyways, an associate of mine named Joker wants you dead and he's a sneaky son of a bitch, so I just want you to be safe. I hear also you're having issues with the Santana Cartel. I hear the bitch who runs the family is vicious but Moreno and June ain't too wise without a puppet master."

"I see."

"I heard about your son's disappearance. I have my people on it, so we say you have a lot going on just to stay awake. From my understanding, there is an assassin in Miami on your trail. Her name's Ayesha; she is the person you need to worry about. She is very deadly. She did a lot of work for Cartel families, and everyone seems scared to death of her, so be careful."

"Thank you, I'll keep that in mind," Ali said, and they talked for a couple more minutes, then went separate ways.

Chapter 15

Key West, FL

"Boss, you have a visitor!" Biggs shouted into Ali's office intercom speaker in his new mansion.

"Who?" Ali stayed sharply because no one really knew he lived here yet.

"Boss, he says he is family and he don't need to give a name. He looks a little crazy. The man got a half face. Do you want us to get him away?" Biggs loved violence. At six foot six, he weighed three hundred pounds—all fat and water weight.

Ali rushed downstairs, knowing the visitor was Jacob.

"Jacob, what the fuck! Come in." Then he told his guard, "Get out the way!" He saw how battered Jacob looked, with dirty clothes, unshaved, and bags under his eye.

"We need to talk in private," Jacob said in a soft voice as Ali led him out back.

"How did you find me?" Ali asked, walking through the kitchen to see his beautiful Haitian maid cooking dinner.

"I am an ex-combat warrior with connection."

"How could I forget?" Ali said, walking downstairs to the lower level backyard where a tennis court was surrounded by a basketball court and the pool area.

"They killed Amina while she was pregnant after we got married. It was Abu Hurayra's son—Isaac. Lucky I was able to kill him, but I'm out for blood."

"I'm sorry, Jacob, somebody got Lil Ali."

"What!" Jacob replied, thinking he misheard him.

"Yeah, somebody kidnapped him but Abu Hurayra's daughter has been helping me put it together because she is very connected."

"Where is she? I am killing everything he loves," Jacob said with pain in his eyes.

"Jacob, please you can't kill or harm her."

"Do you hear how you sound? Do you know how dangerous Ayesha is? Bro, the bitch is ten times worse than me."

"Jacob, she is my wife. I recently fell in love and got remarried. I had to move forward after Laura's death, and Ayesha completes me."

Jacob was lost for words.

"Okay, Ali, just because I love you like a brother I'm leaving her out of this. I'm going back to the Middle East to do a huntdown, and maybe she can help me with some leads—"

As soon as Jacob paused, Ayesha came downstairs in a Alexander McQueen sundress with all types of knives and weapons strapped to her.

"Hey, baby, who is our guest?" she said with her long hair in a ponytail, looking beautiful as the sun hit her glowing skin.

"This is Jacob, he's family," Ali said.

"Nice to meet you, Jacob, you have long résumé in the Middle East," she said, knowing who he was. She was upstairs in the window earlier, watching his every move.

"Likewise, but your father killed my wife, and I'm out for blood. I killed your brother Isaac, and your father is next."

Ayesha looked shocked. Isaac was a great shot, so she couldn't fathom how Jacob killed him.

"I'm sorry to hear that but my father is trying to kill me as well—I guess we're all in the same boat," Ayesha said with a shrug.

"I need your help," Jacob began. "I believe your father is hiding out in Iran in a town called Yazd. Your father is in a forest, I presume."

"It's true he hides somewhere in the Yazd mountains but I do know he will attend the biggest yacht party of the Prime Minister of Iran. I believe his name is—"

"Maulona Yosafzai—yes, I'm familiar with him," Jacob replied.

"My father and he are very close. Their party is held next month—same month every year. It's normally a mask and lace party and the guest list is strictly based on invitation but you have to be wise because they will sniff you out like a bloodhound and kill you. The Prime Minister is a very dirty man."

"Tell me more," Jacob said, and they talked more until he came up with a solid plan.

***

Days Later

South Florida

Ayesha was at a gun range, firing several shots into the target, hitting the bull's-eye each time as police officers were next to her.

She still trained every day, even though lately she was feeling weak and as if she had a stomach virus.

Once she was down, she handed her target sheet to the old white ex-marine sitting in the front her 5K assault rifle, headphones, glasses.

"Holy shit! Fuck me raw—I've never seen a shot like this in years. Who the fuck are you, young lady? Every time you come in here, you amaze me. You got sharp shots—always ninety-nine percent accurate." The white man looked in her colorful bright eyes.

"I'm just a woman not to be fucked up," she said, walking out as the trace phone was ringing in her purse in the Louis Vuitton bag.

Her trace phone was used only for hits. It was her private line.

"Who is this?" she answered the blocked number as two police officers nodded at her, while she walked out to her gray Aston Martin D11

"Hey, sis, or should I call you *a dead bitch*? You should've followed daddy's orders. Now I have to come kill you. Do you prefer knives or guns?"

"Listen, Israel, both of you will need knives and guns, so come prepared when you get off your knees from sucking daddy's dick—homo." Ayesha hung up with a hiss, climbing in her car, playing a Halsey album on her iPod digital car touch screen system

She went to her doctor's office to see what was wrong with her, then she planned to go home.

Chapter 16

North Miami

Ali just came back from checking on his casino which was doing great as he knew it would.

The bulletproof Rolls Royce Ghost was gliding through the streets followed by two SUV trucks full of armed and dangerous Haitians.

Ayesha texted him telling him to come to her condo so she could please him asap; he only prayed it wasn't bad news in disguise.

His driver and favorite bodyguard—Jamel—pulled into the mezzanine level of the condo garage to see all luxury cars from the rich residents.

When his driver parked, Ali put on his Tom Ford blazer, covering his two Desert Eagles in his holsters. He hopped out, looking around the garage cautiously as he made his way to the elevator.

Bloc, Bloc, Bloc, Boc, Boc, Boc, Boc—

Two of Ali's guards took head shots. Ali was the first to shoot back as Mexicans came from all angles of the garage.

"Jamel, cover for me, I'm going to my right," Ali said, as he and Jamel hid behind a BMW X5 truck as the Mexicans were taking out the Haitians one by one with their military style weapons. Ali popped up, shooting two Mexicans in their necks, as they slid behind a 550 Benz, causing one of the guards to take over twenty rounds to the chest.

"Four of them at six o'clock—" Jamel looked in the rearview mirror.

"One, two—one, two—"

Bloc, Bloc, Bloc, Bloc—

Boom, Boom, Boom, Boom, Bloc, Bloc—Ali and Jamel surprised all four Mexicans, killing them with ease. Meanwhile, bullets whizzed past their heads, making them duck again as they saw over ten Mexicans left; whereas their own gunmen were dead, leaving them outnumbered.

"It's too many of them, man, and I'm almost empty!" Jamel cried as they heard an AR-15 assault rifle hit every Mexican who tried to run from Ayesha, but she was hawking them down.

"Ali, can we please go now?" she said, walking around the Benz to see Ali and Jamel out of breath with their heads leaning on the car door.

"Why the fuck are y'all hiding?" she asked.

"The boss just needed a break," Jamel said, getting from the floor, poking his chest out, looking at the BMW truck and Benz which bullets turned into Swiss cheese

"Okay, whatever—can we leave before the police come? We won't be coming back here no more," Ayesha said, climbing into the Rolls Royce. Ali looked pissed, staring at the Mexican lying dead on the floor with his head busted wide open.

"Sorry about that," Ali said, as Jamel pulled off while she placed the AR-15 on the floor.

"Did you see the two guards that ran out of the garage as soon as the shooting started?" she asked.

"It's not the time, Ayesha," Ali said, knowing she was being funny.

"Whatever!"

"What's so important?" Ali said, looking at her red Chanel sweat suit.

"I'm fucking pregnant, asshole!" she said, looking out the window to see a Chinese store, the sight of which made her suddenly desire some Chinese food.

"Oh, my god! Come here, I love you so much," he said, hugging her, then kissing her as she finally smiled. They drove to their home to make sweet love.

***

Guadalajara, Mexico

Joker was in his bed in one of his mansions with two beautiful Mexican women—one named Celeste; the other, Jenny. He slid his index finger beneath Jenny's red thong, feeling her warm gushy pussy as he kissed his lips while she moaned, groaned, and arched her back into his moving finger, following his silent command.

Jenny was a petite dark Mexican, with short brown hair, and big breasts. Celeste was five foot seven, with a pretty face, dark long hair, small tits, tattoos, and a tongue ring.

Jenny started to suck his dick, going crazy, slurping and jerking him until she saw his pre-cum.

"Bend me over and fuck me while I suck her pussy, papi," Celeste said, as she got behind Jenny who was now on all fours with her ass jutted out. Celeste dived in Jenny's deep pussy, as Joker grabbed her hips and rammed his cock in and out of her wet pussy. "Uggghhh—shitttt—Ummmm—" Celeste moaned as she sucked on Jenny's swollen clit.

"I'm cumming," Jenny said, as Celeste's tongue ring did tricks in her pussy.

"Fuck me!" Celeste yelled, as Joker roughly fucked her until she came on his dick, while Jenny came in her mouth.

Joker pulled out, and both women started to suck his hard dick; they took turns, and he closed his eyes, thinking how blessed these young women were for using their brain for something worthy.

Jenny was eager for some dick after she took it out her throat. She nudged Celeste out the way; she wanted her dick time. She climbed on Joker's dick. He leaned back, feeling her wetness drip all over his gut and thighs, gripping her waist.

"Damn! You got some good pussy," Joker said in Spanish, grinning as she rode him up and down, slamming on his dick, hitting her G-spot.

Her body began to tremble in ecstasy as she came hard on his dick. She squeezed her pussy walls on his dick as he came. Meanwhile, Celeste was licking Jenny's asshole and Joker's balls.

"Damn, ma—uggg—ohh—yesss—" Jenny moaned. Then she screamed. "I'm cumminggg again!" she shouted, bouncing up and down.

After some different sex positions, the three were all worn out, and sniffed some lines of coke.

Jenny sniffed a line of coke off Joker's dick, then sucked it wildly as they went for round two. Both women were prostitutes with two different types of STDs—herpes and syphilis. Joker didn't know about their STDs, though

***

Next Day

Joker was in his library, reading an old history book about the war between Mexicans and the Spaniards. It was the Mexican War of Independence, which lasted from 1808 to 1821.

He was worried about D-Bo because the job should have been done. Ali was at hawk point. Joker gave D-Bo some gunmen who were war-ready.

When D-Bo told him about the garage shooting and the attempt on Ali's life, he was pissed, wondering why Ali was still alive.

Joker had to come up with a Plan B. He planned to call Spyder later to brainstorm.

***

Lil Havana, Miami

It was close to 1003 degrees outside today. Everybody was out playing dominos and cards on the blocks.

"'Me telling you, June, there's something missing—she got something going on," Moreno began, referring to Sofia.

"Yeah, but she deals with Rivera, and we have been dealing with him for years; he wouldn't let no shady shit happen under his nose," June replied, sitting inside his stash house in the poverty area where he grew up. "If she crosses us, we kill them both easily."

"Right, but any report on our friend? He is a headache—I can't wait to X him out," Moreno said.

"I'm sure Haitian Boy will show his face—It's such a tender dick, we will be okay," June said, watching the soccer game on a flat screen, as his goons were in the other rooms.

"The student can never be the teacher—I'll show you why," Moreno said, leaving.

Chapter 17

Dade County, FL

Haitian Boy laid in his side bitch's house, hooked up to IV's for two weeks now, but he was getting better. After he was shot, this was the only place he knew would be safe and not have to worry about the police.

Luckily, the two bullets exited through his back. He lost a lot of blood, and would be in a lot of pain for a couple of weeks, but the pain killer she gave him was what did the job.

Lil Snoop sent a crew to check on him every other hour until he was ready to turn the city up again with him.

"Baby, Lil Snoop here!" his older side bitch yelled, as she was on her way to work.

"Damn, nigga, you all cosy under the blankets watching Family Guy," Lil Snoop said, looking at *Family Guy* on TV.

"Shit, bruh, I'm on vacation but what's happening, man?" Haitian Boy said.

"Niggas is waiting on you, cuz."

"I know but I'm still trying to figure out who that black ass nigga was trying to take my head off. It crazy because at first he tried to help a nigga, then next thing I know—the African nigga trying to kill me after he killed my man." Haitian Boy shook his head, grabbing the remote, turning to the Sports Center.

"Hold on—African nigga?"

"Yeah, old buddy had waves and shit—I saw his face clear," Haitian Boy said, as Lil Snoop pulled out his phone, scrolling through some pictures.

"You mean this bull?" Lil Snoop said, passing him his phone with a picture of Ali, Fatal, D-Bo, and Lil Snoop himself. They took the picture two and a half years ago in Vegas.

"Yeah, bruh, on my shoulder—that's him."

"I gotta go holler at Ali. That's his man—or *was*. His name is Fatal. From Brooklyn."

"I'ma kill that nigga after I kill these Cubans."

"Nigga, first you need to get better instead of letting them niggas do a 50 Cent move on you," Lil Snoop said, laughing, walking out.

"Be safe, bruh!" Haitian Boy shouted before the door slammed.

***

D-Bo had been trailing Lil Snoop all day in a Ram pick-up truck. Now he was following him, watching him leave a small house. Presently, he was going into a shopping center, where he parked his Lambo. D-Bo had been waiting for the perfect time. He looked at his watch. It was seven p.m., and darkness had fallen as Lil Snoop ran in a phone store.

"These blacks are going to be hard to kill without going back to jail—they are always around the camera," a Mexican man said, sitting in the back seat of the truck.

"Why don't you shut the fuck up!" D-Bo said, annoyed, watching Lil Snoop diddy-bopp out the store. "It's time, stay in the car—he's alone, so I got it; this is personal." D-Bo jumped out the passenger seat, pulling his Champion hoodie down.

Lil Snoop just paid his phone bill. He saw a call from Ali and answered it on the first ring.

"Fatal is the one who tried to kill Haitian Boy—I just left him," Lil Snoop said, standing outside his car.

"Damn it! Look, I need to meet with you and Butter J."

"I'm on—" was all Lil Snoop said, as he felt the cold steel to his head.

"What's up, bull? Good to see you, nigga, you even got a little tan—who you on the phone with?" D-Bo said, snatching his phone out his hand.

"Who this?" D-Bo shouted but heard nothing, then he looked at the screen to see Ali's name. "Boss man—just the nigga I've been hunting, or you want to say anything to Lil Snoop before I send him on his way? Bull, this feels like a Philly reunion." D-Bo grinned.

"I'ma kill you when I see you," Ali said.

"Yeah, yeah, that's my life story, cuz, but you gotta run," D-Bo said, hanging up, placing the phone into his pocket. "Turn around so I can look you in your eyes."

"Nigga, you gonna talk or handle your business?" Lil Snoop said, seeing people walk past, paying them no mind.

"Okay, gangsta."

"Yeah, I'ma gangsta, bitch ass nigga!" Lil Snoop shouted, as he hogged spit in his face. D-Bo laughed before pulling the trigger three times as people yelled and ran to their cars.

D-Bo ran to the pick-up truck.

***

North Miami

Next Day

Sofia rode through Miami to meet with some business associates. She saw Ali's Rolls Royce Ghost driving through the city with no guards. Sofia saw it was a woman in the back being chauffeured, and she knew it was Ali's Ghost because of the license plate.

The Ghost went to a doctor's office as Sofia watched Ayesha. Jealousy filled her heart because Ayesha was the baddest bitch she had ever seen. She would make a straight bitch turn dyke.

Sofia was on the black Ducati motorcycle, watching as Ayesha walked out the doctor's office forty minutes later with a smile.

The Ghost was on its way to South Miami towards the bridge which was packed with traffic, bumper to bumper.

"Damn this traffic! I hate this bridge, but we are going shopping, and then to the spa right after I take care of this little situation," Ayesha said, looking in the rearview mirror.

"I thought it was only shopping," Jamel said. "Ali's going already mad, we have no guards with us—I can't get fried," he added, exasperated.

"Shut up and drive!" Ayesha said, as she popped out the sunroof with a Tommy gun with 100 shots and a shoulder strap

Tattt-Tatt-Tatt-Tatt-Tatt-Tattt-Tatt—

Ayesha shot at Sofia, hitting her in the thigh. Sofia sent shots back as traffic started to move now.

Ayesha saw Sofia following them since they were at a red light near South Beach. The two were going back and forth. She caught Sofia in the arm as she swerved off the white line while her bike skidded across the yellow line.

She could have finished Sofia off with a headshot, but she chose to let the Puerto Rican bitch live for today. Ali had some explaining to do, though.

"Good driving, Jamel, time to go shopping—and keep that to yourself—I'm not asking you, I'm telling you!" she said turning, up the Keyshia Cole album, singing loud.

Jamel's heart was still racing. He'd never thought a woman so beautiful can be so deadly. He planned to find a new job before the end of the week.

Romell Tukes

Chapter 18

Carol City, Miami

Butter J stood before the fence in front of the trap house, surrounded by goons running in and out the house.

"We're going to find out who did the shit, cuz, Lil Snoop was a brother to me," Haitian Boy told Butter J. "A chick told me she saw a big brown-skinned baldhead nigga with a beard. She said he looked like an out of town nigga." Haitian Boy was telling Butter J what LaLa from Overtown told him, as she saw the whole scene from inside the shopping center nail salon.

"Fuck! I know who it was. I'ma kill that nigga."

"I'm with you, bruh, but first we gotta deal with these Cuban and Puerto Ricans," Haitian Boy replied.

"A'ight, I got a little plan—I'ma holler at you," Butter J said, walking to his Bentley Mulsanne, as a truck full of Ali's goons rolled with him.

Butter J was supposed go back to Philly yesterday. Having just heard about Lil Snoop's death now, he had no choice but to find D-Bo. What he did not understand, though, was his reason for being in Miami

Butter J called Man-Man and put a plan together.

***

Key West, FL

Ayesha wore an all-black strapless Fendi dress with six-inch heels, as her long hair lay on her back. She was preparing a halal meal as she set up the dining room table neatly with candles, table cloth, and dim lights to see the view.

"How did the appointment go? Sorry I couldn't make it, baby, I had to take care of some legal issues but next time I will accompany you to the doctor's," Ali said, as Ayesha brought two plates of food out for them.

"I'm sure you will, but let me explain to you—I'm not a fucking toy or one of your ex's, so don't play with my heart Or I will kill you!" There was a crazy look on Ayesha's face.

"I'ma let that shit slide because you're pregnant," he said, as Ayesha tossed her plate at him, barely missing his face.

"What the fuck has gotten into you!" Ali yelled, now pissed.

"I'ma ask your black ass this question—who the fuck is Sofia Santana, and what does she want with you?" Ayesha said, with a butter knife in her hand, unaware of it stabbing the table.

"What happened?" Ali asked seriously.

"Don't make me ask you again about your bitch. What you trying to protect? I should have killed her but I'm sure she is in enough pain." Ayesha smirked.

"Did you kill her?"

"Wouldn't you love to know? I can't believe this."

"It's a long story, Ayesha."

I have all night," she said, crossing her arms.

Ali started from the beginning when he and Sofia met in middle school and became a couple. He told Ayesha how Sofia robbed him and faked a pregnancy. He explained how she was the daughter of Santana. He explained how she drugged him and raped him, and now he had a daughter.

Ayesha couldn't believe what she was hearing. She prayed it was all lies, but she never knew him for being a liar.

"So you telling me you have a daughter?"

110

"I didn't know until recently." He looked at her, as she leaned her head back.

"Thanks for finally telling me—the bitch could have kill me, asshole!" she shouted.

"I didn't want to push you away or fuck up what we had going on, but I wasn't going to leave you in the blind."

Ayesha stood up. "You can sleep your nasty ass on the couch and leave me alone—I fucking hate you!" she screamed, going upstairs, crying.

Ali went out his backyard and sneaked past his guards to hop in his Porsche 911 Turbo, pulling off quietly.

***

Ali sat down at a waterfront ten minutes away from his home. He and Ayesha came here daily.

He was sitting on the bench, staring into the stars, drinking a bottle of Henny, feeling the liquor hit him strong.

With everything in life going on with his son, the war, marriage and his unborn seed, he felt happiness was slowly being snatched away from him. Everything he loved got close to dying or crossed him.

"Life can't be that rough, bull," a voice said, creeping behind him as Ali continued to drink.

'Nice of you to finally join me, D-Bo."

"You look like shit but I'll make your life easier," D-Bo said, pointing a gun at him as he leaned on the rail.

"I prefer to look like shit than cross my family," Ali replied.

"You think I wanted to deal with the Mexicans? They threatened to kill my family. What would you do if you'd been in that situation?" D-Bo asked, pointing his 357 at his face.

"Death before dishonor—you do the math—but I assume you came to Miami to handle Joker's dirty work like he is your slave master," Ali said with a slur. "Handle your business, I fear Allah only."

D-bo wanted to pull the trigger, but something in him couldn't—because Ali was like a brother to him.

Shots came from all directions, and both men took cover, surprised as Butter J and ten soldiers with dreads tried to rip D-Bo's head off.

D-Bo jumped over the rail into the deep water, as Butter J shot him twice in his leg.

'Shit!" Butter J yelled, shooting up the water, emptying his clip.

"You good?" Butter J asked Ali who was drunk.

"Why? I don't look good?"

"Come on, we out," Butter J said, helping Ali up, never seeing him like this as he placed him in his Porsche and took him home.

Butter J had been following D-Bo for three hours, but he was mad he missed his shot.

Once back at Ali's mansion, he was asleep in the passenger seat until Butter J woke him up.

"Come on, homie," Butter J said, as he saw a gang of security pacing the front, nervous until they saw it was their boss as Butter J helped him into the house.

As soon as they walked into the crib, Ayesha was cursing out a group of guards for letting Ali out of their sight in a time of war.

"Is he okay?" Ayesha said, as Butter J led him into the living room, and she saw how drunk Ali was.

"He's good even though D-Bo almost killed him and he caught him slipping. I never saw him like that; he was lacking big time." Butter J left as Ayesha thanked him.

Ayesha told all the guards to get the fuck out, as she went back in the living room to see Ali knocked out while she went to grab a blanket for him, then she lay next to him.

***

Isfahan, Iran

The large yacht cruised down the Mediterranean Sea as the stars in the dark sky made the sea look unforgettable.

The yacht was 189 feet, with three levels, over twenty rooms, a spa, a ball room, a club, and panic rooms downstairs.

Tonight's event was the biggest of the year, with the most powerful men in the Middle East in attendance. Everybody was masked to conceal their identity because there were all types of crazy shit going on—from drug use, sex, and orgies.

The Prime Minister of Iran always threw the craziest parties, and only a private guest list was allowed on the 27.5 million dollars' yacht.

Jacob was on a speedboat closing in on the yacht's back bumper. Wearing a black and silver mask, he tossed a black rope and ladder in his tuxedo. Once on the first level, he was amazed at how beautiful the yacht was, taking in the wooden panel floors and fancy designer furniture.

Beautiful naked Arabian women passed him with fat rich men, going to private rooms to have fun. Jacob walked into a small club area with disco lights and a DJ playing rave music as people danced and turned up.

The tables all had mountains of coke, meth, and ecstasy all on them, as women sniffed lines of coke and meth. "A rum and coke," Jacob told the bartender who was naked with a nice cute face, perky small breasts and a nice little apple bottom ass. The women didn't wear masks; only the men could hide their identity.

He saw a fat man close to four hundred pounds sitting on the couch, getting head from two cute young women who were no older than sixteen. Then he saw two muscular men running a train on a woman who was screaming. When he looked to his right in the corner, he saw an old woman getting banged from the back while she was bent over sniffing lines of dope.

Jacob received this drink and sipped it slowly, as he finally spotted the Prime Minister near the window talking to a group of men.

The Prime Minister wore a half mask, showing his gray beard and gray white hair. He was very short—just five foot nothing—and he walked bow-legged.

As he watched the scene at the bar, a naked woman approached and she looked white, skinny, with hairy pussy, C-cup tits, and long brown hair.

The woman said nothing as she dropped to her knees and pulled out his dick. When she saw how big it was, she looked back at him, wondering if he was even human.

She sucked his dick, twisting her head, wrapping her lips around, not trying to swallow the most of him, as she couldn't get even half in her mouth.

She just focused on the tip and the sensitive skin areas; the bartender watched and rubbed her clit at the show.

After minutes of slurping, spitting, and jerking, he shot a thick load of semen down her throat.

"I love it," she said, getting off her knees, walking off in her heels. Suddenly, a man grabbed her, bent her over and started to fuck her in her ass, and she took it like a champ.

He saw the Prime Minister Yosafzai walk to the restroom alone out of the club area down the hall. Jacob followed, leaving the bartender horny.

***

Yosafzai was taking a long piss in the bathroom stall as he smelled a strong odor from all the drugs he used coming out.

He was so busy pissing he didn't see the man who'd come into the restroom and locked the door behind him.

Jacob put him in the full nelson choke hold, leaving his small dick hanging out in his zipper

"Where is Abu Hurayra?" Jacob asked while the man was about to pass out.

"Canceled—he canceled," Yosafzai was able to say.

"Too bad," Jacob said, snapping his neck in one swift move, and his body dropped under the sink.

Jacob walked out the bathroom to see the bartender bitch waiting for him naked. He took her to the end of the boat and fucked her over the deck until she couldn't handle it, as her little pussy was bleeding.

Before Jacob left, he broke her neck and tossed her in the sea. Then as he climbed back on his speed boat, he heard loud commotion on the yacht.

They had discovered Yosafzai's body.

Chapter 19

Coahuila de Zaragoza, Mexico

Ole Bay was in his dining room, eating a Mexican meal prepared by his maids, listening to Spyder.

"He sent a crew to Miami to kill Ali—I told him not to do it but he wouldn't listen, Ole Bay," Spyder said, shaking his head.

"Okay, no problem, it will be handled, thank you."

"I just wanted to clear my face. He's a very sneaky person."

"I said, Spyder, thank you, migo—you can go."

"A'ight," Spyder said, leaving the large mansion smiling, happy his plan was coming together. He was sick of being Joker's slave. He put in a lot of work for Joker, and he felt as if he deserved more.

Since Joker wasn't playing fair, he was going to play dirty until everything went into motion.

***

Acapulco, Mexico

"Spyder, where you been? I had a shipment I had to get to the Texas Mafia," Joker said, walking on his farm yard as Joker joined him, surrounded by his guards, pigs, cattle, horses, and hens.

Ravens searched the area for dead flesh which was buried throughout the field.

"I had to go see my daughter."

"Oh, she is back from New York?"

"Ummm, yeah, she just arrived today."

"Okay, good news—I found our rat who been telling Ole Bay our affairs," Joker said, smiling

"Oh, good!" Spyder replied, his body tensed up as they walked in his barn house finally of goons.

'Here he is," Joker said, as his guards moved out of their circle, exposing a Mexican man tied up to a chair. The dude was bleeding badly, barely alive.

When Spyder saw it was their driver, his heart stopped because the man drove him to visit Ole Bay many times.

"Did he speak yet?"

"Nope, we know he been paying Ole Bay visits and then we been beating on him all night," Joker replied, and the man's eyes widened as he started to hum something.

"Can't hear you," Ole Bay said to the man.

Spyder could tell it looked like he was about to rat him out, so he pulled out a pistol.

"He's ready to talk," Joker said. "It was—" the man began, but Spyder's gunshots silenced him.

Boom, Boom, Boom, Boom, Boom. Spyder made the man's blood splatter everywhere all over Joker's white Louis Vuitton suit.

"Damn, Spyder, he was about to talk!"

"Fuck him!" Spyder said, wiping the sweat off his forehead.

***

West Philly

Man-Man was parked outside of D-Bo's family home in a nice middle class neighborhood.

Man-Man brought the twins—Bird and Sauce—with him, as well as Big Face Mob who just returned home from doing ten years in San Quentin State Prison in California.

All four men waited inside the minivan, watching the blue house closely.

"Bird said this nigga pops use to be a model back in the day," Big Face Mob said in his deep voice, grabbing his dick. Big Face Mob looked like Terry Crews from the movie: "Friday After Next". He was big, and he loved to rape men in prison.

"Nigga, what type of weird shit you on, bruh? Man, we about to slide in there, y'all ready?" Man-Man asked, hopping out the van in all black.

***

"Mom, I just want to go out on Saturday with KeKe, and Sunday I'll go to church—I start college soon, cut me some slack—I'm brown now," Anatonnette told her mother at the dinner table, as her stepdad—Joe—just read the TV guide.

Anatonnette was sexy. She had greenish eyes, long brown curly hair which she wore in an afro, and big double D tits with pierced nipples, phat ass, thick thighs and flat stomach. She was a cheerleader, so she was flexible and freaky.

Her mom—Anna—was her twin, just a lot older, but she still had the body and looks.

Joe was an ex fireman and model. He could easily pass for Denzel Washington, but now he was a drunk.

"I understand, baby, but you're still my daughter," her mom said, eating her pasta.

D-Bo took care of his family as a kid. He hustled for them to have a good life, even though Anna had a city job as Santana's assistant.

"I'ma go get a beer," Joe said, getting up.

"What new?" Anatonnette said, fixing her dress which reached up her thick thighs

"What I tell you about being rude?" Anna told her with an evil look.

Seconds later, Joe walked back into the dining room area with his hands in the air, as Big Face Mob's gun was pressed to the back of his head.

"Oh, my god!" Anna shouted in a scary voice.

"Damn, they both wet as hell," Man-Man said, looking at how sexy the mother and daughter were.

"Where D-Bo?" Sauce asked both women who looked nervous.

'We don't fucking know," Anatonnette said with an attitude.

"Twin, she got a mouth on her; close it for me," Man-Man said, and Bird grabbed Anatonnette, then bent her over on the dinner table, grabbing her big soft ass as he lifted her dress to see her pretty pussy. "Damn, baby!" Bird said, pulling his dick out and slowly entering her, making her moan as her pussy was dripping wet.

Her pussy was so wet Bird was enjoying making love to her. He pulled out her tits as his body rocked back and forth.

"Uggghhhh—Ohhhh—" Anatonnette moaned as his curved dick hit her G-spot.

Sauce grabbed Anna, unzipping her pencil skirt to see a big wide ass, as her hairy pussy poked out while he roughly bent her over, fucking the shit out of her. She screamed as he rammed into her dry pussy, almost ripping the skin off his dick.

"Ohhh—Pleaseeeeee—stop!" Anna yelled, as he ripped her dry wall, while tears poured from her eyes.

"Come on, it's time to go," Man-Man said, while Sauce tossed Anna on the floor, as cum that looked like cottage cheese came out her pussy.

"Bird, what's up with you and that chick?" Sauce asked his brother, as Anatonnette got off her knees from sucking dick, hiding behind Bird.

"She with me, bro, I believe she won't say shit—right?" Bird looked at Anatonnette questioningly, and she nodded.

"Okay," Man-Man said, shooting Joe and Anna in the head as Anatonnette screamed with tears.

Without hesitation, he shot his man Big Face Mob in the face twice.

"That nigga was tripping, you ready now?" Sauce asked Man-Man.

"Not yet," he said, shooting Sauce and Bird in the face, killing both men as Anatonnette covered her mouth, crying as her nice tits flapped around with every move.

"Please—you can fuck me too, just let me live," she said, as Man-Man laughed. He shot her seven times in her heart and lungs, and as she collapsed on Bird's body.

Man-Man walked out, still fucked up about what he just saw happened.

Chapter 20

Key West, FL

Ali was still on the hunt for his son, but he was somewhat losing hope even though he knew he was still out there.

Things at home were getting a little better even though he now spent his nights in one of the guest rooms with blue balls since the Sofia situation.

Ali was in his office when Ayesha walked in wearing a gray garment and hijab.

"It's time to pray?" he asked her, looking at his Roger Dubuis $1.3 million watch, knowing this was the only time she spoke to him in his office.

"No, but it's time to put some work in," she said, sitting down as he raised his head from his laptop.

"You're pregnant, what are you talking about?"

"Israel is in town and he always attends the Shahryar Mosque on Friday for Jummah—since childhood" she said.

"I'll handle it," Ali said.

"What! He is my brother; I should be able to kill my own blood."

"You're only allowed to drive, Ayesha, and watch from a distance."

"Okay, perfect—thank you, hubby."

***

North Miami

Israel hated coming to Miami because it was the city of the devil to him. Israel was hard-core Sufi Muslim. So when he saw women walking up and down the block half naked, it made his blood boil.

The mosque was packed today for Jummah service. There were many foreigners in the building listening to Imam Abu Malika from London give his hour sermon.

After the long service, everybody went back to their daily lives and jobs.

Israel was in Miami to find Ayesha. His leads were the CMA Casino, where he'd been looking for the past two days.

Leaving the mosque, it was a very humid hot day outside, as he crossed the street towards the small parking lot where his Audi A8 was parked.

Seven feet away from his car, he saw a shadow—then felt a strong high power electronic choke that made him pass out on the floor.

Ali wore a black garment with a black hijab so he could conceal his face. He stuck a long needle in Israel's neck. He saw his body move, but the tranquilizer he just gave him was sure to take him out for an hour.

A Range Rover and an SUV truck pulled out of their parking spot after watching the whole scene, as two of Ali's guards tossed Israel in the SUV truck.

Ali then hopped in the Range Rover with Ayesha, and they drove to Carol City as if nothing happened.

***

Carol City, Miami

Israel woke up three hours later in a cold, dark, wet warehouse full of copper and metal pipes on racks.

He realized he was tied to a table, stretched out, as he was chained to every angle of the table.

"Hey, brother, As-Salaam-Alaikum, glad to see you woke up—it was so easy to catch you slipping because you keep the same routine," Ayesha said with a cold laugh, slapping Israel in his face.

Israel paid her no mind as he saw Ali at a desk putting something together.

"Daddy is going to kill you when he finds me."

"Shut up! Oh, my god! You're on your last leg and still talking about Daddy. Let's focus on you because you're outta luck." Ayesha turned to Ali. "You're ready, baby?"

Ali handed her a baby chainsaw.

"Good to see you again, Israel, but where is my son?"

Israel just stared back at him, mute.

"Okay, let's play," Ali said, as he started sawing off Israel's right hand fingers.

"Ahhhh!" Israel yelled with tears, as his fingers easily fell on the concrete floor. He was screaming so loud the guards heard him outside.

"You're ready to talk?" Ali asked.

"I don't think he is," Ayesha said, cutting off his other fingers, as he started to feel dizzy.

"Okay—Abu Hurayra had Lil Ali!" he screamed.

"What the fuck!" Ali said, already having a strong feeling it was him because everything led back to him.

"Where is he?" Ayesha asked, a little shocked at her father for going against his own code of honor.

"Iran, in Yazd—at his house in the woods we used to go to."

"A'ight, we're done here, baby," Ayesha said, and Ali stabbed Israel in his leg, chopping it off as he cried and passed out. Ayesha laughed and screwed off his arms and legs, leaving his body mangled. They both put over twenty-nine bullets in his head, turning his face into mashed noodles.

***

Dade County, Miami

Haitian Boy was back to normal after being shot. He was exercising and becoming stronger than ever.

He was in an old Chrysler 300, waiting for June to come out of the barbershop. Haitian Boy owned this very barbershop. Last week Haitian Boy sent his goons to rob three of June's stash houses, and it was the mother lode.

Once they killed his sister and Lil Snoop, he was now heartless and wasn't going to stop until it was completely over.

The Dominicans in Miami were like cousins to the Haitians, so they were all close; they ran every barber shop in the city.

Once Haitian Boy saw June was in the barber chair, he grabbed his double barrel 12 gauge pump, and hopped out as the skyline darkened.

"I tell you, this is going to be the biggest thing Miami has seen in a long time—Miami ain't never seen a club like this—it will be the talk of the city," June told his Dominican barber as the Reggae artiste Ozuna played in the background.

"That's going to be hot—a club, spa, pad, and basement restaurant," his barber said, cutting his hair Caesar-style

There were six other men sitting in the waiting area on the wall as the masked man walked in with a shotgun.

"It's time I gave—" *Boom*! June's brains exploded all over the shop window. The barber was shocked as he already knew who the man with the palm tree dreads was.

Haitian Boy placed a Hermes backpack on the floor with 200K in it. Just before Haitian Boy walked out, the barber gave him a nod of understanding.

"Clean this shit up and get back to work," the head barber stated to his four hairstylists.

***

CMA Casino

Ali sat in his office, trying to map out a plan to get his son back since he knew where he was located now.

Ayesha helped him out with some ideas. He hadn't heard from Jacob, but he knew Jacob was cold-blooded on a hot day in hell.

Butter J and Haitian Boy entered his office, both dripping in designer clothes and ice.

"What's good, bull?" Butter J said, as his WS diamond chain danced.

"My son is alive in Iran."

"Ohhh, man, that's what's up, bruh, so what you trying to do?" Haitian Boy said, showing his diamond grill

"It's not that simple—the most powerful man in the Middle East kidnapped him for whatever reason, but I have to plan this out A to Z," Ali said.

"Damn, bro!" Butter J said as Ali's office phone went off, indicating it was a hidden number.

"Ali, my good friend," the very familiar voice said.

"Where is my son, Abu Hurayra?"

"Daddy—Daddy, come get me, I miss you!" Lil Ali shouted in the phone, almost making him cry.

"I will—"

"Now back to business, I want all of your shares from every casino you have. Karma is a bitch but I will have my lawyer fax all of the legal documents to you sometime next week—and once you sign, we can meet in Weybridge, England, so I can return your son."

"Okay, everything will be handled," Ali replied.

"Also tell my daughter *congratulations* on her marriage," Abu Hurayra said in his mischievous tone.

"Let me make this clear, leave my wife alone."

"Wow! Okay, I'll see you in the UK—and don't sleep on my daughter." Abu Hurayra laughed, hanging up.

"This going to be a long week," Ali said.

Chapter 21

Pompano Beach, FL

D-Bo was in his small apartment in a Mexican neighborhood located in the ghetto.

He was on his couch with his legs wide open, getting head from a Mexican chick with big tits and no ass, but her head game was fire.

"Uhmmmmm!" she moaned, tasting his pre-cum as she was deep-throating his entire length, bobbing up and down, slurping up with her spit as she continued to suck him off.

When he heard about the gruesome killing of his family, he took the news hard. Now he had nothing to live for besides a daughter.

D-Bo swore he would take care of Ali and Joker, then Man-Man was last. He hadn't even been able to sleep since he heard the news.

After he came in her mouth, she swallowed it and wiped his dick off with a warm washcloth as he stood up, showing her pretty face and smile.

D-Bo got dressed in his Palm Angels sweat suit, then he started to pistol-whip the Mexican woman until her body couldn't move. Once she was dead, he tossed her body into the hallway closet with two more dead women he recently did the same thing to.

D-Bo placed ten grams on the table and started to sniff the dope. This was the only way he was able to deal with the loss of his family while he put together a golden plan.

***

Monterrey, Mexico

"You're doing a good job in keeping your eyes on this fool—Emigo. He was never supposed to be treated nice from the beginning. He is a low life." Big Loco was addressing Spyder as they walked in Big Loco's backyard.

"I play my role but I know it's time to have my shine," Spyder said seriously.

"We're all subordinate to a position within the Cartel but no family or men is superior to another. It's a cold game, you can't trust a soul."

Spyder wondered what Big Loco meant, but it was too late.

Boc, Boc, Boc, Boc, Boc—Spyder's body dropped in dog shit, as Big Loco walked off to unleash his pit bull and two wolves he kept in cages behind his shed.

***

Miami, FL

Ayesha rode in the back seat of the red and white Rolls Royce Dawn with Butter J as her personal driver and security, since Ali was in the UK to meet with her father.

"I can't wait until this shit is over so I can go to the beach and look at all them people over there," Ayesha said, looking out her window.

"I feel you—I need a vacation, I want to make Hajj, go to Mecca and find me a foreign Muslim joint super rich," Butter J said, sliding down Broadway St.

"Nigga, please."

With a serious look, Butter J said, "Nah, it's real talk, cuz. I suck at cat and mice games. I can't turn my back on my loved ones. You're a trained killer, you may get off on this type of shit." Just then, he stopped at a red light.

Butter J wanted to get out of the game after everything was over. He was rich and set for life.

"I have a kid on the way, Butter, so I'm thinking differently but Ali just doesn't live a regular life and I refuse to watch harm come to my family."

Butter J hit the gas on the green light to see Moreno with goons surrounding him at a small café shop. He and his goons were in the outdoor section of the café, though. "We gotta make a stop."

"As long as I'm not late for my doctor appointment," Ayesha replied, seeing the Cuban boy with his goons waiting on somebody. She pulled out a Kel-Tec PMR-30 sleek autoloading handgun, and Butter J grabbed his two 9mm handguns, parking across the street.

***

Moreno was waiting for Rivera who was late for the meeting. This was a sign of disrespect for Moreno.

Last week, June's body was found dismembered in a dumpster across town. There was no doubt in his mind Haitian Boy's name was on it.

Sofia was still healing from her gun wounds, so he was handling this war alone, but he planned to fly out to Santa Clara, Cuba after the whole shit died

Bloc, Bloc, Bloc, Bloc, Bloc, Bloc—

"Get down!" Moreno's guards yelled, taking cover, firing back as the window shattered while Ayesha wore a burqa, covering her face and the rest of her. Butter J took out two of Moreno's guards as Ayesha sidestepped bullets, ducking, then she hit three guards in the face.

One of Moreno's gunmen almost took her head off; but luckily, Butter J hit him twice in his chest, and the man's body flipped over the outside glass table,

Ayesha shot another guard in his neck, and she saw Moreno crawling at full speed inside the café which was in chaos, with people yelling and screaming.

Butter J took out another guard who was hiding behind a dead plant, as Ayesha shot Moreno in his butt cheek, making him scream.

Ayesha was about to run inside to finish the job but the police cruiser snapped her out of her trace.

"Freeze, now!" the older white cop yelled.

"Damn!" Butter J shouted, getting on his knees, dropping his gun.

"You get down, missus, put the gun down!"

Ayesha looked at the cop as if he was crazy. She released some shots, hitting the cop four times in his head. She and Butter J raced off across the street, climbing in the Ghost, then she reminded him about her appointment in five minutes. He looked at her like she was crazy, as they passed police cars speeding past them.

Chapter 22

Miami, FL

Haitian Boy drove in his 1970 all-orange Chevelle SS. He just came from a big car show in Dade County the city did every year.

He was on his way to Coconut Grove to visit his baby mother—Amanda—who lived in a nice middle class area outside of Miami.

Amanda was a beautiful Spanish woman, thick, smart, educated, a lawyer, and the mother of his daughter—Ashanti.

His crew tailed him in a black Cadillac SUV on the expressway, as he bobbed his head to the tunes of Young Thug.

He saw an all-gray tinted Mercedes SL Class coupé parked on the side of the road as if it had a flat. What really caught his attention was the beautiful sexy ass Latina woman standing next to it, wearing a tight dress emphasizing her ass.

Haitian Boy pulled up close to her, knowing she needed help, hoping he could also get something in return.

"Excuse me, missus, do you need some help?" Haitian Boy asked, walking up to the woman who looked so much sexier up close, with her pretty colorful eyes, olive skin, big breasts, thick curves, and her manicured nails and toes,

"Yes, I do, thank you for stopping—so many cars just passing me," she said with her Spanish accent.

"Your tire is flat right here," he said, leaning over, posting to the rear left tire.

"I had a feeling—"

"Do you have a spare?"

"I believe so, let me pop the trunk," she said strutting to her driver seat as her ass bounced.

"Damn!" Haitian Boy said, feeling his dick rise, as the trunk popped. "I got it," he said, pulling a spare tire out, sitting it on the ground. As soon as he closed the trunk, he was surprised to see the gun pointed at his face. "Bitch—" *Boc, Boc, Boc.*

The gunshots echoed through the dark highway as his body slumped on the side of the road.

Before the guards were able to hop out, Sofia peppered the Cadillac SUV with bullets, killing all four goons, and she hopped in the Mercedes with a low-air-pressure tire.

A while ago, one of Haitian Boy's guards had met her, trying to fuck her, unaware who she was. They exchanged numbers, and that was how she was able to put a location on his phone, tracking his movements which led her to Haitian Boy.

***

Waybridge, England

This was Ali's first time in the UK, and he had to admit it was beautiful, with a lot historic areas and tourist attractions. He saw a couple of places specializing in antiques, and upscale restaurants and cafés on the streets.

Abu Hurayra and Ali agreed to meet in public at a classy restaurant. Ali only came with Jamel—his driver and bodyguard—as he left his goons at the hotel, while others surrounded the restaurant, acting as tourists doing some sightseeing.

Jamel's phone went off back to back, and he pulled over to answer it.

"Shit! Okay, I'll be sure to let bossman know, damn it!"

"What's up, Jamel?" Ali said, fixing his tie on his black Dior suit

"Someone killed Haitian Boy."

"Fuck! How the hell did that happen?" Ali said, letting out a deep breath.

"I have no clue."

"We'll handle it when we get back," Ali said, as they pulled up to the European restaurant, while he grabbed a briefcase full of the legal documents signing over his casinos to Abu Hurayra for the exchange of Lil Ali.

***

The restaurant was filled with civilians having lunch. He saw Abu Hurayra's goons all over the place, as he walked to the corner where he was sitting.

"Ali, have a seat," Abu Hurayra said in his Louis Vuitton suit, while drinking a cup of coffee. "Would you like some tea or coffee?" he asked Ali, smiling.

"Where is my son?"

"Outside, safe and sound but we will get to that soon; let's go over our business plans," Abu Hurayra said, as Ali pulled a folder out of his Gucci briefcase.

"Talk."

"I told you what I wanted and you also asked me to leave my pregnant daughter out of this and I'm willing to, but that would have been my first grandbaby." Abu Hurayra smirked

Abu Hurayra had ties to Ayesha's private doctor in Miami. Her doctor kept him posted on Ayesha; that's how he found out she was married.

"Leave my wife out of this!"

"I will, Ali, it's about our truce deal now. What type of man will I be if I break a truce?"

135

"Here is everything," Ali said, handing him a folder of documents. Abu scanned through them with a smile.

"Everything is good," he said, waving for his man to bring Lil Ali inside, as both men stared at each other.

Seconds later, Lil Ali came into the restaurant, wearing a little tuxedo. When he saw his father, he ran to him as customers thought the scene was so cute.

"Daddy," Lil Ali said, hugging his father tightly.

"You okay?" Ali said, checking his face, neck, arms for any sign of hurt and abuse.

Ali stood to leave, holding his son's hand.

"Ali, have you seen Israel? It's not like him to not contact me."

"I'll mail him to you," Ali said seriously, walking out the restaurant, as Abu Hurayra had flames coming out his head.

Chapter 23

Months Later

Ayesha's belly looked like a basketball was sitting in her stomach. She was to deliver a baby boy any day now.

Lil Ali was now seven years old, and was very smart for his age. Ayesha cared for him as if he was her own. He couldn't wait until his baby brother was born. He wanted another sibling so bad.

The baby shower was amazing. Ali dropped 2.1 million dollars on the baby shower in this CMA casino ballroom.

Abu Hurayra took all of his Vegas casinos plus the ones the Middle East, except the CMA casino.

Since Haitian Boy's death, Butter J and Dead Eye took over Dade County, and put the city back where it was supposed to be.

Hurricane Rebecca was supposed to hit Key West and Miami today, so the city was shutting down.

Ayesha was looking at her bedroom balcony doors to see the gray clouds and hard rain, the strong winds almost knocking down the palm trees in her backyard. It was a nasty sight as she thought about her future in her silk flower robe.

"Oh, my fucking god!" she shouted, as she felt her water broke; the water leaked down her legs.

"Rudy!" she yelled for one of the house guards.

"Yes?"

"Get the doctor!" she yelled, holding her stomach, wobbling toward the master bathroom.

Ali was out taking care of business at his casino, but luckily he was able to find an in-house doctor willing to live in his guest house just until the baby was due.

Ayesha wanted to have her son at home in a water-filled tub. She heard it was safer that way, and especially today with the storm.

Lil Ali came running into the bathroom, having woken up from his nap, to see her in pain.

"You're okay," he asked with his kid voice.

"Lil Ali, call your father on my phone—Rudy, where the fuck is that doctor!" Ayesha yelled in pain, leaning over on her marble sink.

***

Downtown Miami

Ali just came from closing his casino because the hurricane was supposed to hit hard, and he could tell from the dark rainy skies that the storm was near.

He was walking to his white Ferrari GTC4Lusso, as loud thunder crashed into the lot while the storm wind speed picked up.

Ali answered his phone call from Ayesha, as his guards were behind him and in the front; they all had umbrellas as the 55 mph wind was picking up.

"What wrong, Lil Ali?" he asked, hearing screaming.

"The baby is coming out now, where are you?"

"On my way, tell her I'm coming!" he yelled to his son, hanging up, rushing to the end of the lot.

Rat-Tat-Rat-Tat-Rat—Bloc, Bloc, Bloc—

Shots were flying all over the parking lot, as D-Bo and ten Mexicans swarmed them from the left and right.

Ali and Jamel took out four of them, using the rain to their advantage. Three of Ali's goons got caught slipping, as the Mexicans sneaked up on them from behind.

When Ali saw D-Bo, he shot in his direction, almost hitting him with a headshot as the gun battle turned vicious. Jamel shot one of the Mexicans trying to get to Ali.

"Jamel!" Ali yelled, shooting at the two Mexicans behind him firing a SK rifle that hit Jamel eight times in his back. The shots killed him on the spot, as Ali's guards took down the two Mexicans that killed Jamel. Meanwhile, the rain kept coming down like hardballs.

D-Bo tried to catch Ali off guard. However, two of Ali's guards covered him, shooting towards D-Bo as he hid behind the van.

Ali made it to his Ferrari, and his two gunmen made it to their Yukon truck, racing out the lot, leaving D-Bo and six of his gunmen shooting at them.

When he was out the lot, he saw a black Lotus Evora 400 parked by the light on the side road watching the whole scene.

Ali made eye contact with the driver, recognizing her instantly. Sofia smiled from her car, raising a 40 cal handgun, letting him know he will be seeing her pretty face soon.

***

Key West, FL

Ali made it home in less than fifteen minutes, almost crashing twice because the storm was taking over the roads, making it very hard to see.

Once inside the mansion, guards were everywhere as he dashed upstairs where he heard Ayesha yelling like a mad woman.

Ayesha was laying in the huge Jacuzzi, as the doctor was telling her to push. The doctor wore a lab coat, gloves, a mask, and had all types of hospital material on his side.

"Push, breathe, push, breathe—come, he's almost here!" the white doctor yelled.

"Baby, push," Ali said, holding her hand.

"Oh, shut up!" she yelled at him as Lil Ali stood outside the door, watching from a distance.

After twenty-five minutes of pushing, the baby boy was out and delivered healthy. He weighed eight and a half pounds, with colorful orange complexion, gray eyes, and good silky hair.

"Damn, he is handsome—he looks like us both," Ali said.

"Yeah, he does," Ayesha replied, still in the Jacuzzi.

"I'm running some tests on him—I'll be right back,"' the doctor said.

"What's his name?" Lil Ali asked, now walking towards them.

"Taqjq," Ayesha said.

"Perfect," Ali said.

***

Pompano Beach, FL

Moments after Sofia saw D-Bo and his crew sneak off to Pompano Beach, she'd followed the man who almost took her baby father's life.

She sneaked in D-Bo's building toward the second floor where she saw Mexican gang bangers coming out of apartment *2C.*

Sofia saw a pretty young Mexican woman rushing out of apartment *2C* with a black eye and swollen lips.

"Excuse me, is the big man with the beard in there?" she asked the woman in Spanish. The woman nodded with tears in her eyes, rushing down the hallway.

Sofia made her way to *2C.* She had two vans of gunmen parked a block away. The storm slowed down, so it was starting to clear since the hurricane had passed already.

She knocked on the door to hear a deep voice. When D-Bo snatched the door open, he looked at her as if she was crazy.

"Who the fuck are you?" D-Bo asked, looking her up and down in the pink Chanel dress and heels showing her sexy manicured toes that would make a gangsta suck on.

"I run the Santana Cartel and I want to talk out—if you got time," she said looking at him as he stared at her big juicy breasts shamelessly.

"Oh, yes, come in, I've heard of you, boss lady," he said, smiling, licking his lips as she walked into the dirty, smelly apartment. "How did you find me? And don't mind the mess sitting on the couch," he said, watching her phat ass sway.

"I have my ways but I want us to join forces to get Ali—I could really use your help," she said, looking at the mountain of dope on a mirror with a dollar bill rolled up.

"Okay, I don't mind but first let's get to know each other, two heads are better than one, and I have a big *one*," he said, rubbing her thick thighs.

"Ummmmm, I would love to find out," she said, as he placed his finger in her phat pussy that was dripping wet—as it did all the time.

"Damn, your pussy feels good!"

"It does now, let's see what's packing," she said, pulling out a big, fat, hard dick.

"Oh, wow!" she said, kissing him, as he lifted her dress over her thighs while she climbed on his dick, positioning herself on his massive dick.

"Mmmmmmm—your pussy tight—what the hell—you're a virgin?" he said, releasing her tits and sucked them, as she slowly bounced up and down on his dick, getting a rhythm.

"Uggghhhhh—hmmmmmm—" she moaned, riding his dick like a pro until he came in her. Her pussy was on a different level, he thought to himself.

Five minutes later, she climaxed hard as she called him *Ali*—the wrong name. Luckily, he was so caught up in the best pussy he ever had that he didn't hear her.

Sofia got on her knees, ready to suck some dick.

"Suck this dick—you better swallow, bitch!"

"I do, papi," she said, licking her cum off his dick with no hands as she reached for handgun, unbeknown to D-Bo. Then Sofia shot him in his head seven times before fixing herself up and grabbing her purse.

"That's for my sister Alexandra!" she yelled, leaving. She was waiting to catch D-Bo and Lip Snoop for years once she found out they were responsible for Alexandra's death.

Chapter 24

South Florida

Butter J was in his black on black Cadillac CTS. He had been watching Rivera's every move for the last twelve hours. Now he was at a car dealership trying to buy a blue Ferrari F12 Berlinetta worth $312,000.

Rivera had two guards with him as he approached a black car salesman who was cleaning chrome rims on a AMG Benz coupé that just arrived in stock.

"Excuse me, I want this car here and I want to go for a test drive," Rivera said, pointing at the Ferrari.

"Okay, let me go get the keys," the man said, rushing off, grabbing the keys off the wall inside the showroom, hoping for a big tip and bonus so he could pay off his student loan.

Once in the car, Rivera speeded out the lot, sending the car racing all the way down the main streets. "Sir, I think you just ran a red light," The car salesman said from the passenger side.

"Cash or credit card?" Rivera asked, stopping at the red light on 169th Street, watching two thick Spanish women cross the street with boy shorts on, as their ass was both hanging out.

"Cash with a tip is good."

Boom, Boom, Boom, Boom, Boom, Boom—bullets busted through the glass, killing Rivera and the salesman instantly, leaving both men dead at the light, as the black Cadillac did a U-turn, speeding off.

***

Abu Dhabi, United Arab Emirates

Abu Hurayra's private chopper landed on the landing area of the yacht that was 157 feet and full of armed Arabian guards ready to kill.

Abu Hurayra was escorted to the lower deck area. He admired the beauty of the place as he was led to a medium-size office to see his beautiful younger sister—Hadrat—waiting on him.

Hadrat was thirty-three years old, rich, sexy, petite and brown-skinned. She had thick eyebrows, long black hair, colorful eyes, high cheekbones, and white straight teeth. Single, she was the most dangerous women in Dhabi.

When she saw her sneaky, greedy and shady brother walk in her office, she wanted to vomit; she had a strong dislike for him.

"What the fuck do you want and tell me why I shouldn't feed your ass to the fucking sharks in the Mediterranean Sea? You may not even be worth their while." Her Arabian voice rose to a crescendo. She eyed him while fixing her purple hijab.

"I'm still your brother," he replied, sitting in a recliner leather chair across from her.

"Yes, that's the sad part because I wish you weren't. You're a cold-blooded, self-centered snake. So once again what the fuck do you want?" She tapped her black long manicured nails on her desk.

"I need you to do me a favor—you still owe me one because if it wasn't for me, the evil snake, you wouldn't have this oil trade, tech casinos in Dhabi, and your rich lifestyle. You would be a Muslim wife with four kids, taking orders from a nobody husband and living in poverty!"

144

When she was young, she was kidnapped by a terrorist group leader—Hidayatullah Ziauddin—who was a member of the Tablighion, run by Abu Hurayra.

Abu Hurayra got his sister back by killing Hidayatullah's whole army in a matter of days.

"You plan to hold that shit over my head forever—what type of man does that, so-called brother?" she said, as he laughed.

"I don't plan to but I just like to remind you."

"Just like how you poisoned our parents, killing them for their wealth?" she asked.

"Somewhat, but we're both going to lose money, sis, there is a war going on and we could both lose our stocks and investments if we don't take care of the issues," he said. Now he had her full-blown attention.

Hadrat was all about her empire and business; she refused to let anything or anybody come between her successes. She and her brother had billions of dollars invested together in stock—thanks to their parents' inheritance.

"Who is it?"

"My daughter."

"Not Ayesha, it can't be."

"Yes, she has crossed sides with the enemy; she got married and had a baby with the enemy after I sent her to do a mission."

"I can't believe that. She normally does everything you ask her, shit! I basically raised her. I believe there is more than what you are telling me." Hadrat was shocked because she raised Ayesha like her own daughter in Oman.

"She married a man named Ali and things went left."

"I believe I've heard that name. He's related to Musa, right?"

"Yes, you could say so."

"How did you even enter dealing with the blacks? I've heard they are very dangerous people."

"Business is business," he said, leaving out the part about how he crossed Ali first.

"I will handle my niece and after this I never want to see you again. I will feed you to my poisonous King Cobra snake. Now get the, fuck off my yacht!"

"Will do, thank you for your time," he said, getting up to leave.

"One more thing—if you cross me, I will kill you!" she said seriously, looking him in his cold sneaky eyes.

"You can't kill something that's already dead," he replied with a smile.

"Watch me—" she replied as he left.

***

San Juan, Puerto Rico

Abu Hurayra's chopper landed at the private landing strip, as a Rolls Royce limousine awaited him and his goons so they could be brought to their destination.

Before he planned to go back home, he had to make a pit stop to put his plan in motion.

He and his goons drove through the beautiful city, as gray clouds surrounded the city as if a storm was near.

Lissette Santana was Sofia's older cousin who lived in the capital of Puerto Rico. She also had other homes on the outskirts, but she loved San Juan.

The city had the best beaches, clubs, restaurants, homes, and music. It was like a bigger Miami to meet with so much fun.

146

She ran two hair salons, and she opened a middle/high school for the poor and she was philanthropic to the less-privileged of Puerto Rico.

Growing up in the Santana Cartel who ran Puerto Rico was hard because she lost a lot of family members to violence, drug wars, and area jail.

She was forty-six, with three grown kids who all lived in New York. At her age, she was still beautiful. She had a nice body, long blonde hair, white complexion and hazel eyes.

Lissette agreed to take Sofia's daughter for a while, so she could handle her business affairs in Miami.

Her four-bedroom house was in a nice decent area in San Juan. She loved taking care of Cristal; she was a good girl and quite.

Lissette put on a robe when she heard her doorbell ring at 1:23 p.m. She was just waking up from her long nap because Cristal had her up all night.

"Yes? How may I help you? she said, looking at the three large Arabian men in suits. Before they even replied, they kicked her door in, knocking her five foot four and a hundred and twenty-five pounds' frame on the floor.

Lissette pulled out a pistol from her robe pocket, shooting one of the gunmen in his neck. The other two attacked her, kicking her gun out her hand, beating her up until Abu Hurayra walked inside.

"Damn, nice shot!" Abu Hurayra said, stepping over the dead body.

"What do you want?" she said, as his two men held her down.

"Go to hell, you bitch!" *Boc, Boc, Boc—* "Go get the baby and come on," Abu Hurayra said, looking at Lissette take her last breath, as his men came out with Sofia's daughter who was still asleep as they left.

Abu Hurayra found out Sofia had a baby with Ali. Once he found they were ex-lovers, he put two and two together, and reasoned that the baby had to be Ali's. He knew she was going to Vegas to see him again, so he knew there was a connection somewhere.

After doing his research, he figured Sofia would be a good bait. Now he was up and waiting on Ali.

***

Guadalajara, Mexico

Ole Bay was in one of his five mansions where as he loved to spend a lovely time.

"Sorry to call you on such short notice, but I got good and bad news" Ole Bay said, sitting in his large backyard and his tent, watching horses running around on his 24 acres of land.

Joker had no clue what Ole Bay called him for, but he prayed it was good because his goons and weapons were all out front.

"What's going on?" Joker said, nervously.

"I came up with a better way to traffic drugs. For some reason, we had a little accident last week—one of our planes the Colombians sent us was hijacked, and only few knew about that shipment."

Joker's heart started to race.

"I'm sure we will get to the bottom of it," Joker said, sweating, hoping Ole Bay didn't know he formed a plan with the Colombians to remove the plan.

Ole Bay smiled. "You see, my friend, I have allies with the Colombians for years so I received all my drugs back but you, my friend, aren't so lucky." Before long, forty red dots formed beams, and pointed all over Joker's body as Ole Bay walked off. Then bullets riddled Joker's body from Ole Bay's guards.

Romell Tukes

Chapter 25

Liberty City, Miami

Fatal just touched down back in the *305* after his trip from New Jersey to buy some new arsenal from Abu Saeed—a man Akbar introduced him to before he was killed.

He had been keeping an eye on Butter J since he'd been making a move on Ali who'd been a ghost lately.

Last week, Gorilla and his men in Vegas were all killed. Their bodies were found with money stuffed in their mouths—a sign from the killers to show they were killed over greed.

The thought of Brittany, Kelly and Amber always danced in his head, and the pain was worse than a stab in the back.

He was in a tinted black Dodge Challenger SRT Hellcat in the projects surrounded by killers and drug dealers.

Fatal saw a crackhead walk by every second; he stopped one.

"Look, I got a hundred dollars if you put this in that blue Porsche Carrera GTS exhaust pipes," Fatal said, flashing a small red device.

"Hell, yeah, that Porsche? Pay me first," the toothless dirty man said. Fatal handed him the money and device. The fein did it smooth and fast without being seen, then he rushed off to buy some crack.

***

"I fucking Ace out shit!" Buter J said after shooting dice with a nigga named Avary Lance in the projects. The floor had $200,000 on it as ten niggas were placing bets.

Butter J was the plug in Dade County now—thanks to his New York and Peru plugs—but he still supplied Philly. He even bought a mansion in Coconut Grove worth $7.9 million.

"Hey, yo', I'm out—hit me later," Butter J told his main worker so he could go holler at Dead Eye who was Haitian Boy's cousin.

"A'ight, bruh," AD shouted, and began talking to a hood-rat on the hood of his Bentley Bentayga truck on rims.

Butter J walked towards his Porsche, texting a Spanish bitch he met on Collins Avenue yesterday. She hardly spoke fluent English, but he didn't see that as much of a barrier.

When he got inside his Porsche and pressed the push-to-start button, his car blew up, killing him. The explosion dismembered his body; and as the car went up in flames, people rushed over to him to see some shit they only saw in movies.

Fatal rode past slowly, smiling behind his tints.

One mission complete, he thought.

***

Sarasota, FL

Sofia was sitting on the beach behind her beach house. She was here alone, watching the hard waves crash into each other as nightfall came.

She recently got the news of her daughter's kidnap from Lissette's neighbor who told her she saw four Middle Eastern men invade her cousin's home.

It wasn't hard for Sofia to put the pieces together. She knew about Abu Hurayra's dealing with Ali, but she was confused as to how he connected them both.

Tears flowed down her pretty face, messing up her make-up, as she silently prayed her baby was alive.

She pulled out her phone and called Ali, to only get his voicemail. She tossed the phone in the sand after leaving a message in his voicemail. Minutes later, he called back. She rushed to answer it like a middle school girl wanting her boy crush to call.

"You got the fucking nerve to call me, bitch!" Ali shouted, pissed off.

"Sorry to bother you, Ali, but we need to talk now please—this is very important. It's not about me or you. I just need a minute of your time, Ali." She heard nothing from him but silence. After the pregnant pause, Ali finally spoke.

"Meet me on Biscayne Boulevard at the old boat warehouse at the end. Come alone at nine p.m. Try anything, you'll regret it!" Swiftly, Ali hung up.

***

Hours Later

Sofia pulled into the rocky parking lot in her yellow Lamborghini Aventador to see Ali's old school 1987 Chevy Monte Carlo.

She climbed out in an Alpha and Omega wrap white dress and heels, with her hair in a bun. She looked beautiful. At first, she placed a pistol in her Fendi bag, then she took it out and placed it under her seat.

One thing she knew was, if Ali wanted her dead she would have been gone; she somewhat trusted him.

She walked into the abandoned warehouse to see boat pieces everywhere, mostly rusted and broke boat pieces.

Ali was sitting on a chair in the middle of the floor in a navy blue Armani suit, watching her every move as she approached him.

"Hey," she said sadly, as he gave her an evil look while she sat in the other chair eight feet away from him.

"What is it, Sofia? I have no time for games."

"I killed D-Bo for you," she said.

"You want a cookie, bitch, and I'm sure it was more to do with like Alexandra!" he said rudely.

"Look, I ain't come to argue with you. I came to tell you our daughter was kidnapped by Abu Hurayra."

Ali frowned.

"Fuck! I should have known!" Ali said, banging his fist on the table on his right, causing her to flinch.

"I'ma handle it, but first we have unfinished business," Ali said. pulling out a 9mm Glock and pointing it at her, but she didn't even blink.

"Oh, it's like that? Well, I rather have you kill me than your funny looking bitch." Sofia laughed.

"You crossed me too many times—Karma is the sister of death," Ali said before shooting her eleven times in her head. She died with her eyes wide open as if she deserved it.

Chapter 26

Santa Clara, Cuba

Ayesha rode in silence in a black Lincoln Town Car on her way to the St. John Catholic Church in the heat of Santa Clara—a small beautiful city full of tourists and art galleries.

She looked at her window through her Prada sunglasses, admiring the lovely streets, old-school classic cars, and coconut trees blocking the hot humid heat as pelicans and seagulls flew through the blue skies.

Since the birth of her son, she'd been on mother duty and getting back in shape. She didn't want to be one of those women who lose themselves after a baby.

Right now she had to step in and help Ali with shitty situations with the cartels because they wouldn't give up until he was dead.

The taxi rode up a small hill, as her body was filled with a rush of excitement, feeling the thirst for blood again. Ayesha was now on her 6th passport; traveling became a second life to her, but it was never a vacation. Today she was on an important mission, and her primary target was already located—thanks to an old friend of hers who was a third eye in the sky; he could find anybody in a matter of minutes.

***

Moreno sat in St. John Catholic Church alone in the 5th front row, looking at the Virgin Mary painting.

This was the church he grew up in since he was a kid, so he came to visit it daily just to get peace of mind, especially when he had a lot on his plate.

He had no clue Ali and his crew would be this much of a pain in the ass; he was now losing money and good soldiers.

Never had he been so hard to kill, but he did respect his gangsta so much that he was willing to call a truce. He didn't care about the casinos anymore; he was more concerned about his life.

When he heard about Sofia's body being found in a small river weeks ago, it shocked him but he knew it was only one man powerful enough to take the queen out.

To make matters worse, his wife left him and filed for divorce after she caught her daughter sucking his dick in their bed. When she walked in on them, her daughter was deep-throating him viciously as she was looking at her mother in her eyes.

The head was so good he couldn't stop until he came in her throat after seeing his wife standing there with tears.

"I hope you can say a prayer for me before I kill you," a young woman said softly, as he heard heels clicking on the marble floor coming his way.

When he looked behind him, he saw a sexy Arabian woman with a pair of Louis Vuitton jeans, blouse, and heels with a 50 calibre handgun in her hand.

"Damn!" He was so shocked by her sex appeal he got a hard-on. "Who are you and how did you find me?" he asked, unaware she was the one that shot him in his ass.

"None of your worries."

"You must have killed Sofia?" he asked, but she had a surprised look because she was unaware Sofia was dead.

"I wish it was me who killed her, but I would love to talk and build—so I have to go, playa," she said, firing five hollow tip bullets in his head.

As she was walking out, a friendly priest was walking in the church, giving her a friendly wave.

Ayesha stopped dead in her tracks as he saw her face; and within seconds, she heard the priest scream at the sight of Moreno's blood on the floor, telling her to call the police.

"Okay, I will call the police right away," Ayesha said. Instead of pulling out a phone, she pulled out a blade, and swiftly slit his throat, cutting off his air circulation as blood squirted everywhere, leaving him dead in seconds.

She walked two blocks away, passing a van full of Moreno's guards eying her ass, as she got in the back of the Lincoln Town Car going back to the airport.

***

Key West, FL

Ali was deep asleep in his king-size bed, feeling a little breeze from his open terrace.

He hated sleeping without Ayesha, but he knew she had a life too. She told him she was going to Atlanta to spend the weekend with some old friends.

Ali was a deep sleeper, so he was unaware of the shadow that just climbed in his window after killing four of his guards with a silencer on a Glock 27 outback.

"Wake your bitch ass up!" Fatal yelled, slapping Ali with the butt of his gun, busting his mouth.

Ali jumped up out of his sleep to see a gun trained on him. "How the fuck—"

"Ropes and hooks, fam, what? You thought you was safe in a new mansion? And don't try to yell for them guards downstairs or you're dead—but you're dead, anyway." Fatal smiled.

"Handle your business, nigga, you're still a fuck nigga. I treated you like a brother and now you trying to kill a nigga."

Ali shook his head. Never would he have thought Fatal would've been the one to take his life.

"Cry me a river, you a Philly nigga—you know you can't trust any man especially in the same field as you."

"I'll see you in hell!"

"Maybe—" *Boom, Boom, Boom, Boom!* Ali had shut his eyes in readiness for his body to receive the gunshots like a champ. But then again, he sensed the only pain he was feeling was from his bust lip. So where did those gunshots come from just now? Ali opened his eyes to see Fatal bleeding out the mouth as he fell on the mink rug, dying.

When Ali saw who was behind him with a smoking gun, he rushed to his aid.

Lil Ali handed his father the gun he got from under the bathroom sink. When he heard the man say he was going to kill his dad, he rushed to get the gun that his dad always kept under the sink.

"You okay, daddy?" Lil Ali said, as Ali snatched the gun out of his son's hand, while guards ran in the room to see Fatal in a pool of blood.

"Get him out of here!" he yelled, pointing at Fatal, then he took Lil Ali back to his room.

Lil Ali went right back to sleep as if nothing happened; this scared Ali.

***

Hours Later

In the morning, Ayesha was back. Ali told her the whole Fatal story, and she was pissed. She even put Lil Ali on punishment for a week.

One night, after they were both worn out from hours of sex, Ayesha spoke.

"I heard someone killed Sofia," she said.

Lying naked next her, Ali said, "I heard too."

"What about the baby?"

"I am paying your father a visit soon. I know what he's doing and I'm not going for it. I have a plan."

"My father has a death wish, and I knew after you mailed him Israel's dismantled body, he would take shit to another level until he break you."

"I knew but some things are unbreakable, and I'm one of them."

"I know, but I'm coming with you."

"No—You've been through enough, baby, plus I have help now. Go to sleep before I give you some more of this dick."

"Well—See you tomorrow," she said, turning her sore body around and going to sleep.

Chapter 27

South Philly

Man-Man was blasting 2 Pac's "Hail Mary" in his black Dodge SRT Challenger, as he sped down the expressway, hitting 110 mph.

Earlier today he found out his little brother was gunned down in East Oakland by police on his way to college.

When his little brother was being pulled over, the police saw him pull something out—which was a phone—and they shot him seventeen times.

His little brother was only pulling out his phone to record the police contact, due to all the police killing of innocent bystanders lately.

Man-Man was high off coke as he was on his way to South Jersey to chill with a chick he met at the mall days ago.

Officer Baker was a veteran who'd spent twenty years so far in the police force. He was fifty-six years old, a white racist man with four grown kids.

He saw a Dodge muscle car with dark illegal tints speeding down his highway. He put his sirens on, as he came out the bushes where he hid every night when he was on duty.

Man-Man saw the flashing lights in his rearview mirror, as he slid his Draco onto his lap from under his seat, speeding down the highway.

"Fuck!" he yelled, pouring some coke on the middle of his thumb and index finger. He finally pulled over, rolling down his window, seeing his eyes fire red.

"I thought you never was going to stop; let me have your particulars," Officer Baker said, as a back-up truck pulled up.

"Yes sir," Man-Man said, placing a towel over the Draco that was on his passenger seat.

The cop could tell he was fucked up off something, as he took Man-Man's license and ID, walking off to speak to Officer Morris.

Minutes later, Man-Man saw both officers coming his way, and paranoia took over him—due to all the coke he sniffed up his gorilla nostrils.

"Sir, can you please step out the car, turn off your engine and keep your hands up!" Officer Baker said. Man-Man smiled, thinking about Eric Gray and Michael Brown.

Man-Man opened the door with one hand and used his free hand to let off rounds from his Draco, hitting Office Baker in the skull.

Officer Morris quickly reacted by firing shots into Man-Man's chest, sending his body stumbling back into his car door.

Both men died on the scene before help could arrive.

***

Yazd, Iran

It was close to midnight as the woods was pitch-black, surrounded by wildlife and forest trees.

Abu Hurayra loved peace and quiet instead of city areas where one can get no sleep. His home was well-protected. In the calm cabin house in the middle of nowhere, Abu Hurayra stood over Sofia's beautiful daughter's dead body, feeling guilty for killing her by choking her to death as she suffocated. He was always against killing children, but this was the only way he could get to Ali.

He dreamed of giving Ali and Ayesha both a slow death—both at the same time—but he knew getting his daughter was a death wish and a suicide mission because she was the most dangerous woman out there.

Abu Hurayra went downstairs to get some sleep. He had a long day ahead tomorrow; he could visit his new casinos in Israel and handle all the legal documents with his lawyers to get what he deserves.

He went to sleep, forming a plan for Hadrat after she killed Ayesha—because Hadrat was a snake also.

***

Psst, Psst, Psst, Psst, Psst, Psst, Psst

Jacob took out three guards, leaving their bodies slumped. Hearing the commotion, two guards rushed to the scene, and Jacob shot both guards in their chest with his sniper's rifle.

Jacob was dressed in army war gear with night vision goggles, as he walked stealthily towards the front of the home.

He posted himself on the side of the house to see four guards talking in Arabic about their boss, and how much of a dick he was.

The guards saw red dot lasers on each other's forehead. Before they could pull any stunt, their heads all exploded.

Jacob saw the coast was clear, as he made his way into the dark house that was unlocked.

Once inside, he walked slowly and smoothly with his gun trained on each room as if he was on a special op mission, as he went into all the rooms.

Walking on the wood floors was hard because they would crack and make a noise if you stepped too hard on them.

He made his way upstairs to see a little girl sleeping in her carriage, but when he tried to lift her, the body felt stiff. When he checked the pulse, he realized she was long gone; so he left her, and went on his next mission.

"Hey, Jacob, nice work out there—too bad I have cameras surrounding these areas I own," Abu Hurayra said, pointing a gun at his face as he flicked on the lights.

"You're lucky," was all Jacob could say.

"Have you heard the story of King Pyrrhus and how he used nineteen elephants to defeat the Romans at the Battle of Heraclea in 280 BC? The Romans were unprepared for such a formidable weapon and were promptly decimated. It was all about victory over his opponents."

"Well, that's life," Jacob replied.

Abu Hurayra pulled the trigger on his Ruger to only hear a click, realizing he was out of bullets.

"I came by yesterday when you left, and emptied the only handgun you had in here. Anyway, so long—" *Psst, Psst, Psst, Psst, Psst*—Jacob gave Abu Hurayra series upon series of headshots, making sure he was totally dead.

Jacob took Cristal's dead body with him as he left.

***

Miami, FL

"Daddy, how long do we have to be in Philly?" Lil Ali asked with an attitude.

"Until I say so, that's enough questions," Ali said as he, Lil Ali, Taqjq, and Ayesha rode in a limo to his private jet so they could go stay with his maternal aunt.

"Okay," Lil Ali said, poking out his bottom lip.

"Make sure you take care of your brother and if anything happens, what do you do?' Ayesha asked him sharply.

"Call the number you gave me, I know—I'm not slow— and rule number two: *never call the police*," Lil Ali stated.

"Good and why never call the police?" Ali asked.

"Because they are dirty and corrupted," Lil Ali said, as Ayesha shook her head and Ali laughed.

Ayesha agreed to let the kids stay in Philly until shit died down because it way too risky to keep them around right now with so much going on.

Ali's maternal aunt would be the kids' caretaker while there in Philly; she would watch over them as if they were her own.

Romell Tukes

Chapter 28

Key West, FL

Ali had to go to the CMA Casino while Ayesha went back home. When she pulled into the gates of her estate, she saw no guards. She found this odd, so she was on the alert.

She walked into her mansion in her Fendi sweat suit. When she made it towards the living room, she saw a trail of blood. Before she could even react, she heard the familiar voice, and she froze.

"Don't do it, baby," Hadrat said in her calm voice coming from a blind spot behind the living room wall, with a gun aimed at her face.

"Wow! Surprised to see you," Ayesha said, looking at her beautiful aunt in a Saint Laurent black suit.

"You look thicker now—As far as I recall, you never had much ass," Hadrat said, looking at Ayesha in her sweatpants.

"Thanks—hard work!"

"You have a handsome husband and beautiful children I'm proud of. I just hate I have to kill my favorite niece."

"Let me guess—my father put you up to this shit. He's using you as a pawn until he checkmate!"

"If that's how you would like to put it before I kill you, then yeah," Hadrat said.

"Ummm, fair. At least, let me die with honor in a sword fight. I deserve that, if you ask me."

Hadrat laughed. "You think I'm dumb? You're too crafty with a sword, little girl, but better me killing you than your little sister. You see, my brother is a pussy. He used you, me, everyone, until he eliminates you—and I maybe next, but its life."

"Thanks for the speech," Ayesha said, as blood smeared her Louis Vuitton spike heels from the dead guards Hadrat had dispatched.

"I still love you." Hadrat was about to pull the trigger, but her head exploded off her shoulders like a balloon. She hadn't noticed Jacob's presence at her back as she was focused on Ayesha. The blast that killed her had come from the AR-15 assault rifle Jacob held in his hands.

"I had it under control," Ayesha said, giving him the evil eye as she had a blade under her sleeve.

"No, you didn't, but I came to tell Ali his daughter was killed by your father, but I killed Abu Hurayra so Cristal can rest in peace. Also tell him I'll see him on the other side and I'm sorry, and to take care of my nephew."

Jacob walked out the mansion, leaving her with a confused look as she wondered if he was high.

Ayesha thought about what Hadrat meant by her having a little sister, and the news of her father being killed was too much to bear. She called Ali. He'd just texted her earlier, saying he was near.

***

Jacob was sitting in his black Corvette C7 206 ZRI packed at the bottom area near the mansion gates.

He pulled out a loaded 9mm Beretta, thinking about his life, loved ones, and future that was lonely and cloudy.

Jacob survived bad PTSD which nobody knew about, except Amina, who used to hear him going crazy in his sleep.

He killed hundreds of innocent kids, women, and elderly people just to complete a mission.

There was a monster inside of him that he couldn't control and the only way to release it was to kill him.

Jacob put the pistol to his head in tears, as he pulled the trigger, killing himself.

Ali was outside his gates when he heard the loud gun fire, and he saw the lighting from the gun blast that went off in the Corvette.

Ali hopped out the Yukon truck with his goons to see blood all over the windows, so he was unable to see who was in the car.

When he snatched the door open, Jacob's body fell on the floor. Ali couldn't believe he just killed himself, as his 9mm was still in his hand.

He ran inside the house to see blood and bodies everywhere towards the living room, as Ayesha was sitting on the stairs, zoned out.

***

Hours later, after the house was clean of all the blood and bodies, Ayesha cooked a halal meal. She told Ali the message Jacob left for him, and he was hurt but he knew it comes with the life he lived.

The two talked all night about new plans since all of the real issues were now resolved literally.

Ayesha explained to Ali that she may have a sister that she knew nothing about, and it was driving her crazy as Hadrat's words repeated in her head.

Ali got a call from Ole Bay, and he asked him to meet him asap on his yacht so they could talk. Ali agreed, as Ayesha overhead the name *Ole Bay*; the meeting didn't sit well with her, but she kept it to herself.

***

Monterrey, Mexico

Ole Bay wore Versace slacks and shirt to match, as he was golfing on his lower deck on his 177 foot yacht worth 29.1 million dollars.

He loved golfing and spending time on his yacht in the sea.

"You like golf, kid? It's a good stress reliever," Ole Bay said to Ali, as he sat at the glass table surrounded by Ole Bay's goons watching the waves.

"I golf a couple of times but I'm more of a basketball man."

"I see, I used to be as well while growing up" Ole Bay said.

Ali had no weapons or goons with him. He had to leave his people and guns back at Ole Bay's mansion; it was Ole Bay's policy, but Ali felt naked and uncomfortable.

"I called you out here to tell you Joker is dead—he tried to cross me, so he is the least of your worries," Ole Bay said as Ali overlooked what he just said. "Anyway, I want to tell you a little story before your time," Ole Bay said, pouring himself a glass of liquor.

"Years ago I met a beautiful woman that I grew to love and care for even though she was another man's property. We became lovers and had a little boy. He was my life but I had to play the distant role to avoid trouble because she was now in love with her man. Long story short, my son is killed years later by someone close to him. My son was no angel but he was still my only blood." There was a sad look in Ole Bay's eyes.

"I'm sorry to hear that."

"I had eyes on my son's killer for years and I could never get a hold of him, and he's still out here."

"Damn, I wish I can help."

"You see, Ali, you did enough already because this is the reason why you're here. The woman I was referring to is Mona—your mother—and my son was Haqq, your brother who you killed.

Ali stood up to see twenty H&K MP5 assault rifles pointing at him.

Before Ali could reply, he was on the edge of the yacht as the guards riddled his upper body with bullets. Ali's lifeless body fell into the ocean full of sharks.

When Ole Bay saw blood stain the ocean, and Ali's dead body lying there, he smiled. His mission was now complete.

***

Key West, FL

Ayesha was home all alone sleeping in her safe room that blended in with the wall so nobody would have a clue about the room. This was her favorite room, and all the camera's monitors were in there.

She was sleeping until she heard the alarms go off which made her look at the TV to see over forty Mexicans rushing in her empty house, as well as Arabians. She looked confused.

Ayesha got dressed in her catsuit with a bullet-proof vest and two AR-15s with high coolness on the system.

"I hope they come correct," she said, punching a code into the digital box on the wall that turned off all the lights in the house, as she placed her night vision goggles on and exited the room.

She took out six gunmen outside of the room, then she made her way downstairs, killing ten of them. The killing lasted for twenty minutes until she made it out

Outside in the garage, she killed eight Arabians with ease. Afterwards, she hopped in Ali's Ferrari 488, racing off. She called Ali, and he picked up.

"Ali, where are you?" she shouted in fear for his safety.

"Sorry, Ayesha, Ali is not with us anymore but I'm impressed you made it out. It must be true what they say about you. Well, I'm Ole Bay, nice to finally meet you."

Ayesha was crying, racing down the street.

"You'll be meeting me sooner than you think," she said, hanging up, pulling over to cry and vomit, thinking about revenge.

The End

Submission Guideline

Submit the first three chapters of your completed manuscript to ldpsubmissions@gmail.com, subject line: Your book's title. The manuscript must be in a .doc file and sent as an attachment. Document should be in Times New Roman, double spaced and in size 12 font. Also, provide your synopsis and full contact information. If sending multiple submissions, they must each be in a separate email.

Have a story but no way to send it electronically? You can still submit to LDP/Ca$h Presents. Send in the first three chapters, written or typed, of your completed manuscript to:

LDP: Submissions Dept
Po Box 944
Stockbridge, Ga 30281

DO NOT send original manuscript. Must be a duplicate.

Provide your synopsis and a cover letter containing your full contact information.

Thanks for considering LDP and Ca$h Presents.

Coming Soon from Lock Down Publications/Ca$h Presents

BOW DOWN TO MY GANGSTA

By **Ca$h**

TORN BETWEEN TWO

By **Coffee**

THE STREETS STAINED MY SOUL **II**

By **Marcellus Allen**

BLOOD OF A BOSS **VI**

SHADOWS OF THE GAME II

By **Askari**

LOYAL TO THE GAME **IV**

By **T.J. & Jelissa**

IF LOVING YOU IS WRONG... **III**

By **Jelissa**

TRUE SAVAGE **VII**

MIDNIGHT CARTEL III

DOPE BOY MAGIC IV

CITY OF KINGZ II

By **Chris Green**

BLAST FOR ME **III**

A SAVAGE DOPEBOY III

CUTTHROAT MAFIA III

By **Ghost**

A HUSTLER'S DECEIT III

KILL ZONE **II**

BAE BELONGS TO ME III

A DOPE BOY'S QUEEN III

By **Aryanna**

COKE KINGS V

KING OF THE TRAP II

By **T.J. Edwards**

GORILLAZ IN THE BAY V

3X KRAZY II

De'Kari

THE STREETS ARE CALLING II

Duquie Wilson

KINGPIN KILLAZ IV

STREET KINGS III

PAID IN BLOOD III

CARTEL KILLAZ IV

DOPE GODS III

Hood Rich

SINS OF A HUSTLA II

ASAD

KINGZ OF THE GAME VI

Playa Ray

SLAUGHTER GANG IV

RUTHLESS HEART IV

By **Willie Slaughter**

THE HEART OF A SAVAGE III

By **Jibril Williams**

FUK SHYT II

By **Blakk Diamond**

THE REALEST KILLAZ III

By Tranay Adams

TRAP GOD III

By Troublesome

YAYO IV

GHOST MOB

Stilloan Robinson

KINGPIN DREAMS III

By Paper Boi Rari

CREAM II

By Yolanda Moore

SON OF A DOPE FIEND III

By Renta

FOREVER GANGSTA II

GLOCKS ON SATIN SHEETS III

By Adrian Dulan

LOYALTY AIN'T PROMISED III

By Keith Williams

THE PRICE YOU PAY FOR LOVE II

By Destiny Skai

CONFESSIONS OF A GANGSTA III

By Nicholas Lock

I'M NOTHING WITHOUT HIS LOVE II

SINS OF A THUG II

By Monet Dragun

LIFE OF A SAVAGE IV

MURDA SEASON IV

GANGLAND CARTEL III

By **Romell Tukes**

QUIET MONEY III

THUG LIFE II

By **Trai'Quan**

THE STREETS MADE ME III

By **Larry D. Wright**

THE ULTIMATE SACRIFICE VI

IF YOU CROSS ME ONCE II

ANGEL III

By **Anthony Fields**

FRIEND OR FOE III

By **Mimi**

SAVAGE STORMS II

By **Meesha**

BLOOD ON THE MONEY II

By J-Blunt

THE STREETS WILL NEVER CLOSE II

By K'ajji

NIGHTMARES OF A HUSTLA II

By King Dream

THE WIFEY I USED TO BE II

By Nicole Goosby

IN THE ARM OF HIS BOSS

By Jamila

Available Now

RESTRAINING ORDER **I & II**
By **CA$H & Coffee**
LOVE KNOWS NO BOUNDARIES **I II & III**
By **Coffee**
RAISED AS A GOON I, II, III & IV
BRED BY THE SLUMS I, II, III
BLAST FOR ME I & II
ROTTEN TO THE CORE I II III
A BRONX TALE I, II, III
DUFFEL BAG CARTEL I II III IV
HEARTLESS GOON I II III IV
A SAVAGE DOPEBOY I II
HEARTLESS GOON I II III
DRUG LORDS I II III
CUTTHROAT MAFIA I II
By **Ghost**
LAY IT DOWN **I & II**
LAST OF A DYING BREED
BLOOD STAINS OF A SHOTTA I & II III
By **Jamaica**
LOYAL TO THE GAME I II III
LIFE OF SIN I, II III
By **TJ & Jelissa**
BLOODY COMMAS I & II
SKI MASK CARTEL I II & III

KING OF NEW YORK I II,III IV V

RISE TO POWER I II III

COKE KINGS I II III IV

BORN HEARTLESS I II III IV

KING OF THE TRAP

By **T.J. Edwards**

IF LOVING HIM IS WRONG...I & II

LOVE ME EVEN WHEN IT HURTS I II III

By **Jelissa**

WHEN THE STREETS CLAP BACK I & II III

THE HEART OF A SAVAGE I II

By **Jibril Williams**

A DISTINGUISHED THUG STOLE MY HEART I II & III

LOVE SHOULDN'T HURT I II III IV

RENEGADE BOYS I II III IV

PAID IN KARMA I II III

SAVAGE STORMS

By **Meesha**

A GANGSTER'S CODE I &, II III

A GANGSTER'S SYN I II III

THE SAVAGE LIFE I II III

CHAINED TO THE STREETS I II III

BLOOD ON THE MONEY

By J-Blunt

PUSH IT TO THE LIMIT

By **Bre' Hayes**

BLOOD OF A BOSS **I, II, III, IV, V**

179

SHADOWS OF THE GAME

By **Askari**

THE STREETS BLEED MURDER **I, II & III**

THE HEART OF A GANGSTA I II& III

By **Jerry Jackson**

CUM FOR ME I II III IV V VI

An **LDP Erotica Collaboration**

BRIDE OF A HUSTLA **I II & II**

THE FETTI GIRLS **I, II& III**

CORRUPTED BY A GANGSTA I, II III, IV

BLINDED BY HIS LOVE

THE PRICE YOU PAY FOR LOVE

DOPE GIRL MAGIC I II III

By **Destiny Skai**

WHEN A GOOD GIRL GOES BAD

By **Adrienne**

THE COST OF LOYALTY I II III

By Kweli

A GANGSTER'S REVENGE **I II III & IV**

THE BOSS MAN'S DAUGHTERS I II III IV V

A SAVAGE LOVE **I & II**

BAE BELONGS TO ME I II

A HUSTLER'S DECEIT I, II, III

WHAT BAD BITCHES DO I, II, III

SOUL OF A MONSTER I II III

KILL ZONE

A DOPE BOY'S QUEEN I II

By **Aryanna**

A KINGPIN'S AMBITON

A KINGPIN'S AMBITION **II**

I MURDER FOR THE DOUGH

By **Ambitious**

TRUE SAVAGE I II III IV V VI

DOPE BOY MAGIC I, II, III

MIDNIGHT CARTEL I II

CITY OF KINGZ

By **Chris Green**

A DOPEBOY'S PRAYER

By **Eddie "Wolf" Lee**

THE KING CARTEL **I, II & III**

By **Frank Gresham**

THESE NIGGAS AIN'T LOYAL **I, II & III**

By **Nikki Tee**

GANGSTA SHYT **I II &III**

By **CATO**

THE ULTIMATE BETRAYAL

By **Phoenix**

BOSS'N UP **I , II & III**

By **Royal Nicole**

I LOVE YOU TO DEATH

By Destiny J

I RIDE FOR MY HITTA

I STILL RIDE FOR MY HITTA

By **Misty Holt**

LOVE & CHASIN' PAPER

By **Qay Crockett**

TO DIE IN VAIN

SINS OF A HUSTLA

By **ASAD**

BROOKLYN HUSTLAZ

By **Boogsy Morina**

BROOKLYN ON LOCK I & II

By **Sonovia**

GANGSTA CITY

By **Teddy Duke**

A DRUG KING AND HIS DIAMOND I & II III

A DOPEMAN'S RICHES

HER MAN, MINE'S TOO I, II

CASH MONEY HO'S

THE WIFEY I USED TO BE

By Nicole Goosby

TRAPHOUSE KING **I II & III**

KINGPIN KILLAZ I II III

STREET KINGS I II

PAID IN BLOOD **I II**

CARTEL KILLAZ I II III

DOPE GODS I II

By **Hood Rich**

LIPSTICK KILLAH **I, II, III**

CRIME OF PASSION I II & III

FRIEND OR FOE I II

By **Mimi**

STEADY MOBBN' **I, II, III**

THE STREETS STAINED MY SOUL

By **Marcellus Allen**

WHO SHOT YA **I, II, III**

SON OF A DOPE FIEND I II

Renta

GORILLAZ IN THE BAY **I II III IV**

TEARS OF A GANGSTA I II

3X KRAZY

DE'KARI

TRIGGADALE I II III

Elijah R. Freeman

GOD BLESS THE TRAPPERS I, II, III

THESE SCANDALOUS STREETS I, II, III

FEAR MY GANGSTA I, II, III IV, V

THESE STREETS DON'T LOVE NOBODY I, II

BURY ME A G I, II, III, IV, V

A GANGSTA'S EMPIRE I, II, III, IV

THE DOPEMAN'S BODYGAURD I II

THE REALEST KILLAZ I II

Tranay Adams

THE STREETS ARE CALLING

Duquie Wilson

MARRIED TO A BOSS… I II III

By Destiny Skai & Chris Green

KINGZ OF THE GAME I II III IV V

Playa Ray
SLAUGHTER GANG I II III
RUTHLESS HEART I II III
By Willie Slaughter
FUK SHYT
By Blakk Diamond
DON'T F#CK WITH MY HEART I II
By Linnea
ADDICTED TO THE DRAMA I II III
IN THE ARM OF HIS BOSS II
By Jamila
YAYO I II III
A SHOOTER'S AMBITION I II
By S. Allen
TRAP GOD I II
By Troublesome
FOREVER GANGSTA
GLOCKS ON SATIN SHEETS I II
By Adrian Dulan
TOE TAGZ I II III
By Ah'Million
KINGPIN DREAMS I II
By Paper Boi Rari
CONFESSIONS OF A GANGSTA I II
By Nicholas Lock
I'M NOTHING WITHOUT HIS LOVE
SINS OF A THUG

By Monet Dragun
CAUGHT UP IN THE LIFE I II III
By Robert Baptiste
NEW TO THE GAME I II III
By **Malik D. Rice**
LIFE OF A SAVAGE I II III
A GANGSTA'S QUR'AN I II III
MURDA SEASON I II III
GANGLAND CARTEL I II
By **Romell Tukes**
LOYALTY AIN'T PROMISED I II
By **Keith Williams**
QUIET MONEY I II
THUG LIFE
By **Trai'Quan**
THE STREETS MADE ME I II
By **Larry D. Wright**
THE ULTIMATE SACRIFICE I, II, III, IV, V
KHADIFI
IF YOU CROSS ME ONCE
ANGEL I II
By **Anthony Fields**
THE LIFE OF A HOOD STAR
By Ca$h & Rashia Wilson
THE STREETS WILL NEVER CLOSE
By K'ajji
CREAM

Romell Tukes

By Yolanda Moore
NIGHTMARES OF A HUSTLA
By King Dream

BOOKS BY LDP'S CEO, CA$H

TRUST IN NO MAN

TRUST IN NO MAN 2

TRUST IN NO MAN 3

BONDED BY BLOOD

SHORTY GOT A THUG

THUGS CRY

THUGS CRY 2

THUGS CRY 3

TRUST NO BITCH

TRUST NO BITCH 2

TRUST NO BITCH 3

TIL MY CASKET DROPS

RESTRAINING ORDER

RESTRAINING ORDER 2

IN LOVE WITH A CONVICT

LIFE OF A HOOD STAR

Romell Tukes

www.ingramcontent.com/pod-product-compliance
Lightning Source LLC
Chambersburg PA
CBHW070517260626
47161CB00004B/1576